OVER THE WAVES

by

Marianne Olson

Published in the United States by
Rafter Five Press
P.O. Box 65618, Tucson, AZ 85728

Library of Congress Catalog Card Number: 99-64152
ISBN 0-9673497-0-2

Cover illustration by Pamela Kazal
Copyright © 1999 by Marianne Olson

Printed in the USA by
Morris Publishing
3212 E. Hwy 30
P.O. Box 2110
Kearney, NE 68847
1-800-650-7888

To Grandmother
Sara Lisa Melander

SPECIAL THANKS TO:

Le Clare Steffan for sharing her mother's journal of her trip to Sweden with Sara Lisa in 1914. H. Vedel-Smith, Statens Arkiver Erhvervsarkivet, Århus, Denmark for photos and news accounts of ship travel in 1914. Librarians at Bethany College in Lindsborg, Kansas, Omaha Public Library, and Kungliga Biblioteket, Stockholm, Sweden for help with research. Stig and Violeth Karlson at Klockaregård, Småland, Sweden for showing me where Sara Lisa grew up. The Olson family in Omaha, Nebraska for the many memories shared. Mary Logue for expert editing and critiques. My Tucson critique group: Lynn, Marjorie & Naomi. And especially to Jim for constant support.

1
Summer Plans

June 15, 1914

The voices woke him. Even before he opened his eyes, Joel felt his body stiffen, his senses alert to the angry sounds drifting up from downstairs. Mamma and Pappa were fighting again, spilling out the anger and frustrations that had simmered like leftover coffee all day long. He wished they'd get it over with when they first got mad. But no, "Not in front of the children," he had heard his mother say under her breath. I'm twelve years old, thought Joel. Does she think I don't know?

He kicked off the cotton sheet from his narrow bed and tiptoed into the hall. Down below, a dim light filtered out from under his parents' door. He eased down the narrow stairs leading from his attic room. The wooden floor felt cold under his bare feet even though the air was warm and muggy. Like a cat stalking its prey, he stepped carefully, hoping a creak wouldn't give him away. He knew he shouldn't eavesdrop. But curiosity pulled him on. What could it be this time? Had he done something wrong? Was Pappa still insisting he come work at the shop?

Joel edged closer. They were arguing in Swedish. He used to understand the old country talk better. But that was before he and his sister had decided not to use it anymore. "We're an American family," Linnea had insisted. "We should speak English." Now, as he pressed his ear to the door, he wished he remembered more Swedish.

"....never care what others want," he heard his mother sob. "It's always what *you* want."

Pappa interrupted. "You are stubborn...listen to me.... I know what is best."

"No, Alfred. Not this time. Times are changing and you must change, too."

An icy knot formed in Joel's stomach. They *were* arguing about him, he was sure of it. Had Uncle Karl told Pappa about the job at the paper? For a moment he thought about rushing in and yelling, Stop it! Stop arguing. But instead, he turned, forgetting about creaky steps, and hurried back up to his room in the attic. He thrust his head under his pillow, blocking out the voices, blocking out his hopes for the best summer job ever.

Morning arrived with the aroma of fresh baking bread. The memory of last night's argument permeated the air with the scent of anise and rye. Whenever Mamma was angry or upset, she baked bread. Joel thought she baked an awful lot of bread

2

lately. Much more than their little family of four could use.

He squinted at the clock by his bed. "Drat! I'm late!" he sputtered. He threw on his work clothes, splashed water on his face from the basin on the dresser and thudded down the stairs, two steps at a time. He should have been at Pappa's tailoring shop an hour ago. Now he was late, probably in trouble again. The idea of working in that dingy old place grated on him. School was out. Freedom beckoned like an unexplored trail through the woods. If he had to work this summer, why couldn't it be at the job he really wanted? He could be selling papers from his own stand, or running errands for the press room, like Uncle Karl had offered. At least he'd be outside. Not stuck indoors with two stuffy old men and their scratchy old suits.

In the kitchen, he nearly collided with Mamma carrying two brown loaves, hot from the oven.

"For heaven's sake, Joel!" She hustled to the table, her longs skirts swishing across the floor. She turned each pan over, letting the steaming bread fall onto a rack to cool. "Why are you still here? Pappa left long ago."

Joel grabbed a bottle of milk from the icebox and poured himself a glass. "Do I have to go to the shop today? Uncle Karl said I should see him at the paper."

Mamma frowned. With her blond hair pulled tight into a bun, her narrow face looked pinched and sour. She floured the bread board again and plopped a fresh mountain of dough down, sending puffs of white across the kitchen table.

3

"You already have a job. You must not pester your Uncle Karl."

He groaned, rolling his eyes at the ceiling. "Just because Pappa started as an apprentice tailor, why do I have to?"

Mamma's gray eyes flashed. "Do not speak in that rude manner, Joel. I will not have it."

Joel bit back his reply and watched his mother knead in silence. Her fists gouged the sticky wad, her slender fingers pulling the edges across again as she thrust her weight—and anger—into the dough.

The kneading done, she pulled the dough apart into four balls. Flour-covered hands quickly shaped and patted them into small loaves. "We want so much for you, Joel. For both you and Linnea."

"I know, Mamma, but..."

"Your father has worked hard to build up his business. You are so lucky to have someone teach you a trade. I envy you."

"Why?"

"Because you are young. And a man. You will have so many opportunities in your life. More than I could even hope for."

"What do you hope for, Mamma?"

A small smile flickered for a moment on her face. Her hand wiped away a stray wisp of hair, leaving a streak of flour on her cheek. "You will laugh."

Joel reached across the table, pinched off a bit of raw dough and popped it in his mouth. "No, I won't. Tell me."

"Linnea is grown, eighteen now. You—you are not far behind. I would like to go to work, to earn some extra money."

4

Joel couldn't imagine his mother as a shop girl. "What does Pappa think?"

Mamma eased the four loaves into pans, covering them with a dish towel. "He will not consider it. Not yet, anyway."

The two fell silent. Mamma usually kept her ideas hidden inside. It was new, having her share them. Music from the piano lesson in the parlor took over. Joel heard Linnea, keeping time while her student picked her way through a tune. "One-two-three-four, one-two-three-four." The tick-tock of the metronome reminded him he was late. Like it or not, he had leave. He grabbed an apple and slipped out the door.

At the corner of Cass Street, he hopped on the streetcar and headed downtown. As they bumped and clanged along, he wondered how he could get Pappa to see things his way. He practiced a little speech in his head:

"I know you want me to follow in your footsteps. And I think tailoring's a fine trade. But I'm not good with my hands like you are. I'm better at writing. Even my teacher, Mr. Wedeking, said I had a 'real flair for exposition.' I want a job like Uncle Karl has at the *Omaha World-Herald*. He gets to go where the action is—train wrecks, fires, and such. Remember last year, the Easter Sunday tornado? I went with him to south Omaha to see the damage. Uncle Karl interviewed people and took notes. Remember the stories in the papers? That's my dream—to write for a newspaper."

Now, if he could just make him listen.

When the noisy streetcar lurched to a stop, he jumped off, crossing Farnam Street to where the tiny

5

shop sat nestled between the Danish bakery and the pharmacy. Gold lettering on the window read:
Alfred Peterson, Merchant Tailor
Fine Men's Suits & Coats
Made to Order
As he pushed the door open, a tiny bell jingled. Inside, the peppery smell of wool and silk tickled his nose. Bolts of dark material leaned like tall books on the shelves. Pappa's helper, a white-haired old Swede named Magnus, looked up.

"He's in the back," he muttered and went back to cutting cloth.

Joel found his father hunched over his roll-top desk, adding columns in his order book. He was small in build, but as stubborn and strong-willed as a bear. His fierce dark eyes always made Joel squirm. So Joel focused his attention on Pappa's elegant handlebar mustache and the deep dimple in his chin. They didn't seem quite so gruff.

"Good. You are finally here." Pappa put down his pen and pointed to a dark suit draped over the chair. "Try it on. It is time you start wearing long pants like a grown man."

Joel stood in front of a tall mirror as his father helped him into the almost-finished suit. The suit was a nice surprise. Joel had expected to wear knickers instead of long pants for a while longer, at least until he turned thirteen. The suit made him look older, more like Pappa. They had the same dark hair and eyes, same dimple in the chin. He puffed out his chest trying to look grown up.

"Stand still!"

"It itches."

6

"I can fix that. Now be still."

As his father stuck pins in the cuffs and added chalk marks, Joel felt his stomach tighten. A voice inside urged, Go ahead and ask him. It's now or never. He took a deep breath.

"Did you always want to be a tailor?"

Pappa smiled. "No. I wanted to be a fisherman, like my father. But I was not strong enough for that work." He helped Joel out of his coat and took it over to the work table. He sat down, cross-legged, with the coat draped over his lap. The needle and thread swam along the hem like a fish darting between the waves. "Lucky for me, I learned a trade instead," he continued. "When the chance came to go to America, I was ready."

"How old were you when you left?"

"About your age."

"Didn't your parents want you to stay?"

"*Ja*, they did. But they knew I would have a better life in America." He stood up and poked around in a clutter of button boxes. "I want things better for you, too. Working here, you will not have to start from scratch like I did."

Joel gulped. Here was his chance. "But what if I want to do something else?"

Mr. Peterson turned and peered at his son over his glasses. "And what might that be?"

"I want to write. Be a reporter for the news-paper."

His father threw the coat on the table. "Bah! You will starve doing that. Here you have a solid business waiting for you." He spread his arms out as if offering Joel a grand present.

7

"But I'm not good with my hands like you are. I'm better at—"

Pappa waved him off. "I will teach you! You are too young for such big decisions."

Anger flashed inside Joel as his words tumbled out. "But you were old enough! You just said you came to America at my age. That was a big decision, wasn't it?"

A scowl darkened Pappa's face. "That was different. There was no other work in Sweden for me. Do you think it was easy to leave my family and home? To come alone to a strange land where I did not know the language?" He sank down in his chair by the desk, shaking his head. "You disappoint me, Joel. You take the job I offer and throw it back like a fish that is too small."

Joel stared at his shoes, feeling his face grow warm. He hadn't meant to hurt his father's feelings. He wished he could take back the words. Say them differently. A lump stuck in his throat. But deep inside he knew he was right. Newspapers were the future. Tailor-made clothes were the past. Stores already carried ready made suits, and they cost a lot less, too.

Pappa turned and picked up his needle and thread. "Enough said. While I finish with your coat, see if you can give Magnus a hand out front."

There must be another way to show him, Joel thought. To argue with Pappa was like turning a stone into water. His speech hadn't come out at all like he'd planned. How could he get out of working at Pappa's shop?

Some bright idea had better come to him soon or his dream job would slip away. The rest of the morning he folded and sorted scraps of material, going over all the things he should and shouldn't have said.

2
The Letter

At the end of the day, Joel and Pappa rode the streetcar home in icy silence. They found Mamma in the dining room, dabbing her gray eyes with a hanky. A letter lay open on the table. Joel recognized his grandfather's bold, curly hand and the dark red stamp on the envelope from Sweden. Darn those letters! thought Joel. They always made Mamma sad. But today she looked like she'd lost her best friend.

"What is this?" asked Pappa. "Has someone died?"

Mamma shook her head and handed him the letter. "No. Not yet, anyway."

Linnea, her round face pouting in sympathy, stroked Mamma's shoulder.

Pappa motioned to the table. "Everyone sit. We see what the letter says." He took out his wire glasses, cleared his throat and started reading in Swedish.

Solgården
May 20, 1914

Dearest Daughter Annali,
Health and happiness we wish for you! Please forgive us for taking so long to answer your welcome letter which arrived last month. We are happy to read that you are in good health and for that we must thank God. Here we are not blessed with such good health. Your mother's eyes are worse and she is now almost blind. I go slower each year. But we get along and help each other.

Thank you for the Christmas money you sent to us. You must not think we are as poor as when you left us, dear daughter. The Good Lord takes care of us. Soon it will be time for this life to be over. Last year I turned seventy-six and your mother is now seventy. She sends you her warmest greetings. Her one wish is to see you one more time in life. If only that were possible! But she sees you in her heart and is happy for you, dear daughter. Someday we will see you again in Heaven and that will be a day of great Joy.

I must tell you now that our apple trees are beautiful! Spring has come and they are full of blossoms. We should have a good crop. Now I must stop writing. Greet the family. We are in God's hands. Write soon.

Your father,
Elof Johansson

Pappa folded the letter and slipped it back into the envelope. No one spoke. For Joel, Grandma and

Grandpa were odd characters he'd never met, living in a strange and faraway land. They didn't seem like flesh and blood people. He only knew them from the dozens of photos Mamma kept on the piano. He studied Mamma's face. Tears glistened in her eyes as she bit her lip, trying to keep from crying.

"*Ja,* it is good to hear from the old country," said Pappa with a sigh. He started to get up, but Mamma grabbed his arm.

"Wait. I have something to say."

Pappa sat down softly and just stared at her. It wasn't like Mamma to tell Pappa what to do.

"It is time I go home, Alfred."

"Back to Sweden?" Pappa shook his head. "I can not leave the shop now. You know summer is my busiest season."

"Then I will go alone," said Mamma, her jaw set in decision. "It has been thirty-four years since I saw my home and my family. If I do not go now, I may never see them again."

Linnea busied herself ladling out yellow pea soup. "It will be fine, Pappa. I can take care of things here while Mamma's gone. I have my piano lessons to give, but I'll still have time for running the house."

Pappa tucked his napkin under his chin. "We will talk about it later."

Joel knew that meant no.

Gloomy tension hung over the table. Linnea jabbered on about her new piano student. No one commented, so she, too, fell silent. Mamma ate little, fiddling nervously with her spoon. Finally, she broke the ice.

"I want you all to know I am going home."

Pappa swiped his napkin across his mouth and shook his head. "I do not see how it can be done, Annali. Not all by yourself."

Mamma glared at him. "Alfred, you forget. Like you, I came over all by myself. And then I was only twelve. I can manage now at forty-six."

Good for you, Mamma! thought Joel.

Pappa stroked his mustache, lost in thought. Mamma sat there, her back erect, daring him to speak. When she chose to be stubborn, no one could match her. Joel had learned that many times when he'd tried to get out of doing chores or practicing his violin lessons.

Ideas stirred in his brain, glowing like coals. Imagine—a steamship across the Atlantic! Train rides and faraway places to see. Mamma was right. She should go see her parents again. But all alone? Before he realized what he was doing, Joel jumped up.

"Pappa, why not send me with her?"

His father looked up as if coming out of a dream. His eyes grew wide as the idea sank in. Bam! He slapped the table, making the dishes jump. "*Ja!* That is the answer. If you see where we came from, the kind of life we left, then you will understand why I have worked so hard. You will know why I want so much for you."

Mamma let a smile spread across her face, her victory won. "Think, Joel! You can see where I was born and finally meet your grandparents."

Pappa got up and paced the room, his hands thrust deep in his pockets. He seemed relieved instead of angry. "You will go together with Mamma

13

on this trip. It will be a chance to learn a few things. Prove that you are old enough for making big decisions. Then when you come home, we talk again about jobs."

Joel let Pappa's challenge sink in. If he went away, he'd lose his chance for a summer job at the paper. But much more was at stake. His whole future might depend on how this trip went. He set his jaw in decision. *I'll show him. When this trip is done, he'll have to let me go my own way.*

3
Thunder On the Rails

July 1, 1914

Joel awoke in a cold sweat. Thunder boomers crashed overhead. He darted over to the window and peered out into the storm. A flash of lightning lit up his small attic room, turning night into day. He jumped back and counted the seconds between flash and boom. One-one thousand, two-one thousand, three-one thou—Craaak! He prayed for the storm to stop. It didn't. Rain pelted the roof like a million tiny marbles. Why did it have to storm today? This was the day they had to leave for Sweden.

It had been a busy two weeks planning for the trip. Pappa had arranged to get Mamma and Joel included in a tour group heading for Sweden. Someone had canceled and they got their places. Mamma bustled around the house, jabbering to herself in Swedish as she got things ready. Gone were the stern looks and sharp scoldings Joel had grown used to from her. She acted like a caged bird who suddenly noticed the door was open and she could fly away.

They didn't own an automobile, so a taxi took them to Union Station. On the way, Mamma rattled off lists of things Pappa should do while they were gone. He nodded and assured her everything would be all right. At the train depot, they dashed inside as harried porters scrambled for the luggage.

Heavy, humid air filled the huge ticket hall. Several friends had braved the stormy weather to see them off with flowers and gifts for the trip. Uncle Karl came, too. He held out a dollar to Joel.

"What's this?" asked Joel.

"Your contest winnings!"

In all the hustle and hurry about the trip, Joel had forgotten all about the contest. Each week the *World-Herald* had a riddle on the Children's Page. One week the riddle was: When is a boat like a knife? That was easy. When it's a cutter. But to win the one-dollar prize, he had to send in his answer plus a short story. His went like this:

One night, deep in a dark, dark forest, a band of cutthroat pirates gathered around a fire. As golden sparks flew up into the inky sky, the pirate captain turned to his men and yelled, "Somebody tell me a story!" He pulled his sword from its scabbard and waved it at a trembling, one-eyed sailor. "You there! Tell me a story. And make it a long one or I'll chop off your head!"

The one-eyed sailor stared into the flames and then began his tale:

"One night, deep in a dark, dark forest, a band of cutthroat pirates gathered around a fire..."

The following Sunday, Joel scanned the page, looking for his name. And there it was, bold as brass: "Joel Peterson Wins for His Endless Story." He'd held it up for Pappa to see.

"Look, I'm in the paper! I won a dollar for my story!"

Mr. Peterson took the page, read, then handed it back to him. "*Ja*. That is your name all right. But the story.... What does it mean?"

"It's the kind that goes on and on. It's a story with no ending."

"Hmmm," Pappa muttered and went back to reading the Swedish paper.

Joel had hoped Pappa would be just a little impressed. A whole dollar was a lot of money!

Uncle Karl stuffed the crisp dollar in Joel's coat pocket. "Come and see me when you get back. We'll find some job for you at the paper. Maybe as a printer's helper." From under his own coat he drew out a package wrapped in paper.

"Open it. It's for your trip."

Inside, Joel found a journal bound in brown leather with fine lined paper. "Wow, thanks Uncle Karl."

"Take notes, Joel. Lots of notes. Remember, everyone has a story to tell. Keep your eyes and ears open. Write about your adventures in this. I'll look forward to reading it when you get back. "

Uncle Karl then gathered Joel and his parents together. "Not every day a person goes to Europe!" he said as he snapped their photo.

"Will our picture be in the paper?" asked Joel.

"You betcha! Front page, probably."

"Neat!"

Uncle Karl turned to Pappa. "I'm surprised you would send your wife and son abroad just now, Alfred."

Pappa huffed. "And why not?"

"Things could get messy. The Austrian archduke and his wife were assassinated in Bosnia this weekend you know."

Pappa nodded. "*Ja, ja.* I know. Read all about it. But Annali and Joel are heading for Sweden, not Sarajevo. The good Lord will take care of them."

When it came time, Pappa hurried Mamma and Joel down to track level where steam billowed from the hissing engines. To Joel, it looked like a huge dragon come to carry away him to far off adventures.

They found their car and climbed aboard. While Mamma settled in, Pappa took Joel out to the passageway for a talk.

"I am counting on you, son." His hand grasped Joel's shoulder firmly. "You behave yourself like a gentleman. See that your mother is provided for."

"I will. I'll take care of everything."

Pappa pulled something from his pocket and pressed it into Joel's hand. It was cool and smooth.

"I will miss your birthday while you are gone. So here is your present now."

Joel opened the cover of the silver watch and watched the second hand make its sweep past the numbers.

"Thank you Pappa!"

18

After more hugs, Pappa stepped out on to the platform and waved goodbye. At 6:05—according to the new watch—the conductor yelled, "All aboard!" Over the screech of the train, Joel heard more thunder, giving them a noisy send-off into the pouring rain.

4
Sailing Away

July 2, 1914

Dear Uncle Karl,

I've never kept a journal before, so I will do the best I can. We spent one night in Chicago and then took the Baltimore & Ohio train to the east coast. I explored the train from one end to the other. The last car was a fancy "club car." They wouldn't let me in. Mamma and I had lunch in the dining car. But I like the toilets best. I can see the tracks go by thru the hole!

Two days later, they arrived in New York—New Jersey, actually—where their ship was docked. After spending the night in a small hotel, they hailed a taxi and headed for the pier.

It was the Fourth of July and the pier was packed with taxis, people, carriages, and mountains of luggage. Travelers hugged friends who had come to see them off. Joel bought a small American flag from a vendor. A brass band tooted marches by John Phillip Sousa. Porters pushed through the crowds with carts piled high with trunks while dozens of seagulls squawked farewell overhead.

Huge red and white flags of Denmark welcomed them on board their ship, the *Oscar II*. A single black smokestack rose from the center of the ship between two slender masts fore and aft. Clutching their small bags, Joel and his mother followed the steward down the corridor to their cabin. Joel glanced right and left, trying to take everything in at once. The steward, a tall Dane with a ruddy face, chatted over his shoulder about the ship.

"I'm sure you will find everything you need here," he announced with polished pride. "We have three dining rooms, a music room with a piano, a library, parlors for visiting and playing cards.

"How about life boats? Are there enough?" Joel asked. Memories of the *Titanic's* sinking were fresh in his mind.

"More than enough, sir," replied the steward. "Of course, it isn't likely we'll have to use them."

No, they didn't expect to use them on the *Titanic*, either, thought Joel with a bit of panic. It had only been two years since it sank taking more than 1,500 people to the bottom of the sea. He'd read all about it in the *World-Herald*. Now he wished he didn't know so much about sinking ships and people dying in icy waters.

Pappa had hoped to get them first-class tickets, but Mamma had told him she didn't care.

"After all, I came over in steerage, remember. One big room, with everybody shoved together like sardines. We will be just fine in second-class."

But when Joel saw how tiny their cabin was, he wished Pappa had gotten them first-class. Two bunk beds nestled on one wall with railings that were supposed to keep them from falling out. Opposite the door sat a wash basin on a small vanity table. A narrow shelf and a row of pegs were all they had for clothes. Everything was bolted down securely.

First thing, Joel climbed to the top bunk and peered out the tiny porthole. All he could see was a dark chunk of the pier.

"It's not like home sweet home, is it?"

Mamma patted her bed. "It is just fine, Joel. Come. We can unpack later. We go now and say goodbye to New York."

Outside, it seemed everyone else had the same idea. Ladies clutching bouquets of flowers pushed toward the rails to wave to friends and family on the pier. The air was peppered with different languages: German, Norwegian, Swedish and Danish.

As they shoved off, the steamer gave out a long, deep hooooooot-hooooooot that echoed all the way down in Joel's stomach.

"When's dinner?" he yelled to Mamma over the noise. "I'm starving!" But she was busy waving farewell and didn't answer.

To get a better view, he climbed up on a life boat, balancing his feet on the canvass covered edge. Over the rail he could see the tugs helping the steamer nose its way down the Hudson River. By the time it reached the Statue of Liberty, they pulled back and the steamer was on its own. Joel's heart swelled with pride when he saw Miss Liberty on her little island. He waved at her and yelled, "We'll be back soon!"

A gruff voice called up to him. "Get down, boy!"

Joel glanced down and saw one of the crew scowling at him. He eased himself off the life boat and back on the deck.

"Just getting a good look—"

"Stay off the life boats. They're not toys for boys to play on," said the man. He turned and marched off.

Joel bristled at the idea he was still considered a 'boy'. His stomach lurched. Was that hunger nagging him again? He felt dizzy. The ship had reached open sea and had begun to pitch with the swells. A sour taste reached his mouth. No. That wasn't hunger, it was seasickness.

5

The Girl with the Red Hair

July 7, 1914

Mamma also stayed in bed seasick for three days. Joel felt woozy for a while. But soon he had his sea legs and showed up for every meal. Every day he took a few rolls and some soup back to the cabin for Mamma. He thought she still looked awful peaked.

"Don't you want to walk around a while in the fresh air?"

"No, no. I might be sick again. I best stay here for now. But you go, my little goose. Go."

Joel welcomed the chance to get out of that closet-sized cabin and explore the steamer from stem to stern. He took along his journal and jotted down anything that seemed important.

Counted 25 life boats. Hope that's enough. Heard people talking about the Titanic again. Had a life boat drill last night. Then we had dancing and music

music on the deck. Helped crew hang paper lanterns and flags.

Met Jon. He works in wireless room sending messages. He speaks real good English—spent two years on his brother's farm in Wisconsin. He showed me—

Something made him look up. A girl, about his age, stood by the railing, her arms hugging her body tight against the wind. She looked so frail, Joel feared she'd be blown overboard. Her hair, the color of embers in a fire, whipped across her face. He wanted to reach out and touch the curls, but his hands felt numb.

Suddenly, she turned and looked right at him and smiled. Then she went back to staring at the sea. He felt his face grow warm and considered running back to the cabin, but found his legs had turned to stone. I ought to say something to her, he thought. But what? Finally, she spoke first.

"Did you see those whales out there?"

"No...uh... How many?"

"The mate said there were five of them. Can you imagine?"

His brain was a total blank. He couldn't imagine anything.

"Where are you from?" she asked.

"Oh...Omaha," he stammered. "And you?"

"Brooklyn, in New York."

"Lucky you! I wanted to see some of New York before we boarded the ship. There wasn't time."

She paused, pushing her hair away from her face, revealing a sprinkling of freckles on her cheeks. "It's not so great. We're moving away, back to Norway."

"To stay?"

"Yes. We have family there, in Christiania."

Joel didn't think he'd like living anywhere but in America. He wondered what would make her leave. "What does your father do?"

She looked away, the smile gone from her face. "He's dead."

"Oh...I'm sorry." Drat! Why did he always ask too many questions? But he wanted to know more. "What happened?"

"It was an accident. He worked on the docks." She turned and faced the sea again. A tear glistened in the corner of her eye.

"Did you come from Norway?"

"My parents did. I was born in New York."

"And now you're leaving..."

"I didn't want to. But Mother wants to go back."

"My mother is going back, too. To Sweden. But just for a visit." He fumbled with his journal, wondering what to do next. He held out his hand. "My name is Joel Peterson."

She shook his hand and smiled. "Kari Berg. Nice to meet you. I noticed you writing in your book. What about?"

"Just some notes on the trip, so I don't forget." He tucked the journal under his arm. Plenty of time to write later.

"Want to walk around?" he asked.

"Sure. It's cold standing still."

They walked quietly a while, inhaling the salty air. In spite of the cold, sunshine bathed the deck and glittered on the waves. Off in the distance, mountains of dark clouds piled up on the horizon. Their steps echoed the steady chug-chug of the engines as the ship plowed through the waves. They stopped and read the signs posted by the lounge. One had instructions for a lifeboat drill. Another warned passengers of card sharks.

"Card sharks?" Kari asked, casting a worried glance out to sea. "Are there sharks out there?"

"No, I think it means card players. Gamblers."

"Oh, I see." Kari stuck her hands in her coat pockets and marched on ahead of him.

He ran to catch up with her. "Wait! What will you do in Christiania?"

Kari turned, skipping backwards a few steps. "Stay with an uncle. He's offered Mother a job."

"That's good." He stopped. "Hey, I have an idea. Do you want to play shuffleboard?"

"Maybe later. I'd better go check on Mother," said Kari. "She's been terribly sick. I'm worried about her."

He nodded. "My mother, too. Though Mamma says it's better being sick in second class than in steerage."

Kari frowned, gathering her thin coat around her. "Yes. I'm sure it must be."

She turned abruptly and headed toward the stairway door leading to third class. Then it hit him. Like most of the ship's passengers, Kari and her mother were probably traveling in steerage. Sometimes Joel, you have mush for brains!

6
Funeral at Sea

July 8, 1914

During the night, a storm rolled in and tossed the steamer around like a toy. One minute Joel was asleep in his bunk, and the next he was hanging from the edge, ready to drop. Mamma grabbed his legs and pulled him down beside her. They held on to each other, watching shoes and clothing dance across the floor. Waves pounded the sides of the ship making it groan and creak.

"We'll be okay, Mamma."

"*Herre Gud!* Dear God!" she cried. The ship lurched upward, then dropped again, thudding into the waves.

For three hours they rode the stormy sea as if it were a bucking bronco. Even after it calmed down, Joel could hear the rain lashing at the porthole.

Morning dawned, cold and gray, as exhausted passengers stumbled down to breakfast, greeting their friends with relief. Fresh coffee and hot pecan rolls made the rounds as everyone shared stories about the storm.

"...fell right on my face, I did..."

"...woke up screaming. I actually thought we were doomed!"

"Heard someone call for the doctor..."

"...slept right through it!"

Joel went out, threading his way down one level and along the corridors to the third class dining room. He poked his head in the door, scanning the long tables for Kari. She wasn't there. He wanted to apologize for that thoughtless remark yesterday. He climbed back out to the promenade deck. Off to the left, he saw a flash of red hair. The sound of arguing voices drew him closer.

"No, no. I won't let you!" Kari yelled.

A big man in a white uniform bent toward her, holding her by the arms. Joel figured it must be the captain. He couldn't hear what they said, but he saw Kari's shoulders slump in defeat. What could she be arguing about with the captain? he wondered.

The captain led Kari into the music lounge. Joel followed at a distance. The girl collapsed into a big leather chair and put her head in her hands. After giving her a pat on the shoulder, the captain went his way.

Joel wasn't sure this was any of his business, but Kari looked like she needed a friend. He edged closer.

"Hey...What's the matter?"

She looked up, startled. When she saw him, she burst into tears. Her face, red and puffy, showed how much she had been crying.

"Oh, Joel. It's awful, just awful," she sobbed.

"What happened?"

"It's Mother. She died last night. The doctor said it was appendicitis. We thought it was only sea-sickness."

"Kari, that's terrible. I'm so sorry." He reached into his pocket, found a hanky, and gave it to her.

She blew her nose. "Th-thanks."

"What was the captain saying to you?"

"That's the worst part. He's going to bury her at sea."

"At sea? Why?"

"He says we're too far from land to keep a body. He's going to have the service this afternoon and then...drop her into the water!" New tears welled up and spilled down her cheeks.

Joel knelt down in front of her, holding her hand. He couldn't imagine what it must be like to lose a parent, and Kari had lost both. She was all alone now, on a ship in the middle of the ocean.

"Kari, what will you do?"

"I don't know. Mother had her heart set on going home to Norway. Now she can't even be buried there. I guess I should send word to my uncle."

"Come with me. I know the guy in the wireless room. He'll help you send it."

Joel wanted to keep her busy so she wouldn't cry all the time. He remembered when his little brother had died from the flu, Mamma fought back by cleaning the whole house from top to bottom until she was too exhausted to cry.

As they made their way to the wireless room, Kari jabbered about all the plans she and her mother had made. Didn't she understand how much all those plans had changed? Jon, the wireless operator, offered his condolences and sent her message to Christiania.

Confused and sad, Kari went back to her cabin. Joel couldn't solve all her problems, but there was one thing he could do for her. From the bartender he borrowed an empty cigar box and started to make his rounds.

At three o'clock the steamer came to a dead stop in the water. It was odd not hearing the constant pounding of the engines. Hundreds of passengers gathered on the third class deck for the service.

Kari's mother now rested in a closed wooden coffin, draped in the Norwegian flag. Someone had placed a small bouquet of flowers on top. One of the passengers, Reverend Lundquist, led the service. Mamma and Joel stood next to Kari as the minister gave a short talk about God, Heaven, and Eternal Life. Then they sang the Swedish hymn, "Children of the Heavenly Father." Joel felt his mother grab his hand and squeeze it tight. She always cried when she heard that song, remembering the three children she had lost to Eternal Life.

Six crewmen helped lower the coffin over the railing by ropes. Kari stood still as if made of ice, clutching a red woolen scarf. But when the box disappeared into the dark waters, she turned and ran out of the crowd.

Worried about what she might do next, Joel ran after her. Down along the decks, past the life boats, Kari didn't stop until she got to the ship's stern.

There was nowhere else left to run. She paused, then flung the red scarf overboard.

"Mother!" she yelled, as it fluttered down and floated on the waves.

Joel edged up quietly behind her. "Kari," he whispered.

She sank down by the railing and stared into the swirling waters. The captain had restarted the engines and the ship was once again moving.

"Why did she do this to me, Joel? She drags me all the way out here and then..."

He put his arms around her thin shoulders and felt her body shake with sobs.

"Wh-what will I do now?"

"Come on. Let's go," he said.

After walking her back to her cabin, he headed for the dining room to beg a sandwich for her. But when he brought it to her, she wouldn't take it. First thing the next morning, he checked on her again. She looked much better. Tired, but better. But tears came again when he handed her the cigar box full of money the passengers had given to help her out.

7
The Land of the Midnight Sun

July 14, 1914

Day eleven. Finally we see land. At first I thought there were dark turtles floating out there. But they were islands. Scotland! It felt good to see land again. I never realized how huge the ocean was. Now we are close to Norway. The mountains rise straight out of the sea. Deep fjords cut into the coastline. I counted four long waterfalls spilling down the cliffs. Small villages cling to the coastline. Kari told me trolls live in the mountains. I wonder if I'll get to see one?

That afternoon, Kari and Joel quit playing their shuffleboard game to drink in the view. Since the funeral, she'd spent most of her time with Joel and his mother. It was as if she'd "adopted" them as family. But Joel couldn't really think of her as a sister. Seeing the coastline of Norway reminded him they'd soon have to say goodbye.

"Nice to see land again, isn't it?" he asked.

"It's grand! And so familiar. Mother described it perfectly. I only wish she could have seen it again!"

"What about your uncle here? Do you know him?"

"Hardly. Uncle Ivar wrote now and then. He and Mother were never very close. But now—he's the only family I have. I'll have to take what I can get."

"You're braver than I would be."

Kari smiled and shook her red curls. "Mother used to say, 'When you've got your back to the mountains and your face to the sea, you have to be tough.' Now I understand what she meant."

"How will you to talk to your uncle? Do you speak Norwegian?"

"Sure. It's a lot like Swedish. We speak—spoke it at home all the time."

"Same at my house. But last year my sister Linnea and I decided we'd only use English. Now Mamma and Pappa think they're safe when they talk Swede in front of us. They think we've forgotten. We act dumb so we can eavesdrop."

"You're sneaky, Joel Peterson!"

He half closed his eyes and tilted his head back.

"I like the word 'clever' better."

Kari's hand flew to her mouth, stifling a laugh.

By evening, the steamer headed up Christiania Fjord. It should have been dark by then, but a sunset glow had painted the sky orange. They had arrived in the Land of the Midnight Sun.

Kari had gone back to her cabin to pack while Joel wandered the decks feeling glum. On the second-class deck he found Mamma, wrapped in shawls and busy knitting.

"I had forgotten about the summer sun," she said when he came near. "It made it so hard to sleep at night. The sun went down, and then in a short while, it was up again."

Joel sat down beside her. "Kari's packing up. I don't think she's looking forward to staying with her uncle."

"Yes, poor girl." Mamma counted her stitches. "It is good you were her friend in this hard time."

"Yeah." He tried to figure out what he felt for Kari. He'd never really 'liked' a girl before. And he couldn't understand why being with her made him feel so good and so awful at the same time. He'd have to ask Uncle Karl about that when he got back.

The *Oscar II* docked in Christiania at 5 A.M. but the sun shone as bright as mid-day. Even at that early hour, the people had turned out to welcome the ship. Kari met Joel and his mother by the rail, a small suitcase in hand.

"Will you stay with me until I find my uncle?" Kari asked.

"Of course, dear," said Mamma.

Joel scanned the crowd of people, not knowing how they'd find a person they'd never seen. He spotted a burly man with a bushy beard as red as Kari's hair.

"How about him?" he asked, pointing to the bearded man.

As soon as they disembarked, Red Beard rushed forward, arms outstretched.

"*Velkommen,* my little Kari, welcome!" He scooped her off the ground in his big bear arms. "I know you from your picture. You look just like your mother."

Flustered by this greeting, Kari struggled to get down. "Uncle Ivar, this is Mrs. Alfred Peterson and her son Joel from Omaha, Nebraska."

Uncle Ivar shook hands with them. "Happy to meet you," he said in near-perfect English. "I learn English so maybe someday I go to America, too! Come. Your trunks won't be unloaded for a while yet. We'll go have a drink to welcome you home."

"A drink?" Mamma gasped. "At this hour?"

"A little brandy?"

"But the poor girl has just lost her mother!"

Uncle Ivar waved his arms in surrender. "You are right. We will toast my dear sister, too."

"Perhaps Mrs. Peterson would like some coffee, instead?" Kari said.

"Yes, some hot coffee would be fine."

The city of Christiania embraced the harbor with a fortress perched on a hill on one side, and businesses and homes on the other sides. Uncle Ivar led them through a small park to a restaurant called Café Bryggan. It was closed. But out of his pocket came a key that opened the door.

"My own little place," he said, stepping aside as they filed into the restaurant.

Kari glanced around the large room cluttered with wooden tables and chairs. Down a short hallway, the stairs led up to a second level. A fishy smell hung in the air. Paintings of sailors and ships lined the walls and net-like curtains covered the windows, letting in a dim light.

"This is where Mother would have worked," Kari whispered to Joel. "Maybe I will have her job now."

Uncle Ivar brought out steaming mugs of coffee for everyone. He poured a hefty portion of brandy into his own.

"*Skoal!*" he said, raising his mug high.

"To your new home, Kari," Joel said, clinking his mug to hers.

Kari hesitated. "It's hard to think of this as home. But I guess for now, it is."

Uncle Ivar gave her a whack on the back, nearly knocking her over. "You will like it here, girl! And I could sure use some help with the customers. Ha! Sometimes they get so drunk, I drag them out and toss them in the harbor."

Mamma shook her head but kept quiet. Joel could tell from her expression she didn't like this loud, brandy-swilling man. Homemade root beer was the only strong drink ever in their house.

"Maybe we should go now, Joel," said Mamma, giving Kari a sympathetic look. "She needs to get settled."

Panic filled Kari's eyes. "Can't you stay a little longer?"

Joel sensed Kari felt more at home with them than with her uncle. He wanted to grab her hand and dash out the door.

Mamma got up. "No, we must be on our way. Please write to us, Kari dear. Let us know how you are."

Kari scribbled her address on a paper for Joel and he did the same for her.

"I'll come to the pier at three to see you off," Kari said, giving his hand a squeeze.

After a week and a half on the sea, it felt good to be on solid ground again. Mamma and Joel hiked up Karl Johansgate and past the royal palace. Down street after street they walked, looking in store windows. Joel noticed right away how old everything looked. The gray stone buildings were streaked with soot. The streets were not paved with smooth bricks or asphalt like in Omaha. Here, rounded cobblestones made crossing the street a challenge. At a small market, they bought cheese and bread. Then they headed up to a hillside park with a view of the harbor.

After a picnic lunch, Mamma stretched out on the cool grass, yawning.

"Why am I so tired?"

Joel checked his watch. "Because we've been up all night. Only there wasn't any night. That midnight sun is confusing!"

"Do I have time for a little nap?"

"Plenty of time."

While Mamma rested, Joel lay back, watching the fluffy clouds float by overhead. He wondered what Kari was doing at that moment. Was she thinking about him, too? His heart felt like someone had shoved it under a rock. He closed his eyes and tried to see Kari's face, freckles and all.

It seemed like they had only been there a few minutes when a long, deep hooooot-hooooot jolted Joel awake. He sat up and peered toward the harbor. He checked his watch again, his mind racing. How could it be? It wasn't possible! Their ship was sailing off without them!

8
A Change in Plans

July 15, 1914

"*Nej, nej!*" Mamma paced about, twisting her gloves. "Joel, how could we miss our ship?"

"I don't understand. We had three more hours!" He kept staring at his watch as if the answer would appear on the face like magic. He thought back on the day. They had left the ship early this morning, visited with Kari and her uncle, walked through the town, had a picnic, rested in the sun.

"Oh, no!" he groaned. "How could I have been so stupid? It's all my fault."

"How so?"

"I haven't changed the time on my watch since I met Kari on the ship. And with the sun up at all hours, I got mixed up."

"Oh, Joel!" Mamma flashed a scolding look at him. "Your head has been in the clouds ever since you met that girl!" She took a deep breath and calmed

39

down. "Come. We go to the pier and see what to do now."

Even at a fast pace, it took them about an hour to reach the harbor. They went straight to the steamship office.

"Ship go down the fjord now," the clerk tried to explain in halting English. "You can take mail boat later." He spread out a map on the counter, tracing the mail boat's route down the coast. "Tomorrow it come to Copenhagen."

"But our baggage...," Mamma protested.

"It leave the ship in Copenhagen."

Mamma held her head in her hands, rubbing at the temples. "What should we do? If only Alfred were here!"

Joel studied the map, tracing routes on land and sea. After the last stop in Copenhagen, they had planned on taking a ferry across to Sweden. Then a train to Vetlanda, near Mamma's home. Since he'd made such a mess of things, he had to figure something out. Pappa had counted on him.

"What about a train? Is there a train from Christiania to here?" He pointed to a tiny dot on the map.

"*Ja*, the train go..." The clerk turned to check the clock on the wall behind him. "...it go in one hour."

"Let's do that, Mamma. We can send for our baggage later."

"Can we?"

"*Ja, ja*. No problem. I send message to ship."

"Speaking of messages," Joel said, "can you give this to the girl in Café Bryggan?" He tore out a sheet of paper from his notebook and dashed off a quick note to Kari. His stupid mistake had also cost him the chance to see her again. There was no time to waste now. He had to get Mamma on the way again.

The train from Christiania crossed the border at Charlottenberg, winding through dense forests, rocky mountains, and farmlands dotted with lakes. Mamma sat with her nose pressed against the window, devouring the sights of her homeland. Every now and then she would grab Joel by the arm, saying, "Look! Look how nice the little farms are. They have not changed!"

"You're right," he would answer, teasing her. "They look just the same." How could he know if they had changed or not? It was all new to him.

While Mamma stared out the window, Joel got out his journal and jotted down the strange names of the towns they passed: Lilleström, Kil, Degerfors. How different this all was from the flat prairies of Nebraska. He made a sketch of a purple and orange sunset on Lake Vänern. A tingly feeling crept up his arm as he drew. Was there some magic to this land they had entered?

After spending one night in Hallsberg, they caught the early morning train south to Vetlanda. There, they hired a driver and a wagon to take them the last few miles to Mamma's home.

9
The Stray Bird

July 16, 1914

The driver, a wizened old man with a gray beard and scraggly hair, eyed the weary travelers with suspicion.

"You come from America, do you?" he asked in Swedish.

"Home for a visit," replied Mamma.

"Ah, the stray bird has come back to dark Småland," the old man said. He clicked his tongue and the horse trotted on.

Joel tapped Mamma's arm. "What does he mean? 'Stray bird'?"

"He must mean me, since I left for America."

"And 'dark Småland'?"

"We are in the province of Småland now. It is called dark because....Well, look around."

One glance gave him the answer. The dirt road they traveled wound through dense forests of pine and fir. At times, the branches knit together overhead, nearly blocking out all the sunlight. Joel felt he had arrived in a land of mossy, green giants. He thought of the troll stories Kari had told him on the ship. Were there trolls in the forest now, watching them with their beady eyes?

The miles dragged on. Joel's back ached from sleeping in strange beds. And now this endless, bumpy ride. He glanced over at Mamma sitting erect in her rumpled, black traveling dress with its long sleeves and high collar. She must have been just as tired, but she didn't show it. The deeper they rode into this alien land, the more she smiled and hummed to herself. But Joel began to wonder if soon they'd come to the end of the world.

Finally, the wagon burst out of the darkness and into the sun-dappled countryside. Waves of grass and wildflowers beckoned from farmlands where the forest had been cleared away. Mamma pointed to the thick stone walls marking the borders.

"Those walls are all around every farm. Before we could plant anything, we had to dig up the rocks. The land seemed to grow rocks so we made walls from them," she explained.

They crossed a stone bridge marking the start of the village of Stentorp. It wasn't much. A post office, a general store, a blacksmith, and the tiny red building where Mamma had first gone to school.

At an old wooden church, the wagon turned onto a narrow lane. It led up a hill to a cluster of buildings called Solgården, or Sunny Farm. In the center, Joel spied the blue and yellow Swedish flag flapping from a tall pole. And just under it, the good old Stars and Stripes to welcome them.

Mamma squeezed his hand, her eyes brimming with tears.

"*Nu är vi hemma,*" she whispered. "Now we are home."

As the wagon pulled into the yard, two rumpled old people came out from the red wooden house to greet them. Grandpa looked exactly like the photo sitting on the piano at home. White hair set off the black Sunday frock coat, his neck ringed with a white collar, like a preacher. He guided a tiny ragdoll woman, her head wrapped in a white peasant scarf, over to the wagon. Joel hopped off and helped Mamma down. In two steps she embraced her parents. She tried to speak but her voice choked on the words.

Grandma's wrinkled hands reached up to pat Mamma's face, now wet with tears.

"Is this you, Annali, all grown up?"

"Home at last." Mamma folded her mother into her arms, hugging her, both of them rocking together and sobbing for several minutes.

Joel shook Grandpa's hand, bowing deeply from the waist like Mamma had taught him. "So nice to meet you, Grandpa," Joel said in his best Swedish.

"Ha! What a fine and proper son you have, Annali," cried Grandpa. "And he can talk Swedish!" He wiggled his bushy caterpillar eyebrows at Joel.

"Just for you, Grandpa."

Grandma stretched her arms toward Joel. "Come, come. Let me give you a hug." Her eyes, frosted gray from blindness, did not fix on him. She pressed him close against her billowy apron. It smelled of yeast and cinnamon.

Grandpa took Mamma's hand and danced a little jig around her, his white hair bouncing as he went.

"Look at you! What a fine American lady you have become! All dressed up and wearing a fancy hat...," he said with a laugh.

"No, not a fine lady. A tired lady," said Mamma, making him stop. "But at last we are here. We have been on the way for seventeen days."

Grandma shook her head in disbelief. "Think! You have come home all the way from America, from *America*. Dearest God!"

Joel wondered if his grandparents had ever traveled anywhere beyond Småland. America seemed as far away as the moon to them.

Grandpa checked the wagon.

"No trunks?"

"It's a long story. They will come later," said Mamma.

"Then let's go in for coffee," he said.

"Here, hold my hand, Annali," said Grandma, stroking Mamma's hands. "It's been so long. Are you really here?"

Joel was surprised to feel a lump form in his throat. It was odd for him to see Mamma as somebody's child. She had always been Mother, Mamma, Mrs. Peterson. Suddenly, she was Annali, the daughter, the stray bird come home to the nest.

He scanned the farmyard and buildings. Everything seemed smaller than he'd imagined it would be. Solgården consisted of a squat wooden house with a chimney in the center. Just behind it, he could see the apple trees Grandpa wrote about. Across the yard was a long wooden barn, a wood shed, and an outhouse covered with blooming lilacs. Like most of the farms they had passed on the road, the buildings were painted a dull red with white trim at the doors and windows. A lacy white lattice work decorated the entrance to the house. He was about to follow the others inside when a skinny boy about eight came running out of the barn, scattering the chickens. He wore dark blue overalls and wooden shoes. Spiky blond hair stuck out from his blue cap.

"Come see my horse!" he called, grabbing Joel by the arm and pulling him into the sweet, stinky darkness of the barn.

Joel stumbled after him, wondering what kind of muck he was stepping in. Who was this kid, anyway? The boy pulled him past some squealy pigs, stopping at the last stall.

"Look! Isn't he beautiful?" He pointed to a sturdy brown farm horse with a white blaze on his forehead. "His name is Pelle. I get to groom him the whole time I'm here at Grandpa's. You're Joel, aren't you?"

Before he could answer, the boy added, "I'm Axel. Come on!" and bolted out the door.

10
Cotton Around The Heart

At the entry to the house, Axel paused and kicked off his muddy wooden clogs. Joel sat on a narrow bench in the stoop and pulled off his good boots, now caked with mud. Raincoats, fishing gear, shoes, old newspapers and buckets sprouted in all the corners around him.

Axel ducked into the cozy warmth of the old house, beckoning Joel to follow.

"We can't get mud on Grandma's memories," he said, pointing to the colorful rag rug on the floor.

"Memories?"

"See that blue stripe there? That's my old shirt. I tore it in the forest and Grandma cut it up for her weaving. She can't see it, but she remembers it."

Joel looked across the cluttered living room. A huge wooden loom filled one corner. A basket with balls of rag strips rested on the floor next to it. The rest of the room boasted a crazy mixed-up decor. A pillow embroidered with a Swedish Bible verse shared the sofa with an American flag pillow. The lamp in the corner sported a cowboy on the lampshade. On the wall hung framed pictures of King Gustaf of Sweden and Abraham Lincoln.

Axel pulled him over to a small table crowded with dozens of family photos.

"Here's you!" he said, pointing to the photo taken at Skoglund's Studios last year.

How strange, thought Joel, to come into a place he'd never been before and see his own mug looking back at him. Next to the photos was a copy of *Omaha Posten.* Joel picked it up, feeling a wave of homesickness. Mamma must have sent copies of Omaha's Swedish newspaper on to her family.

Joel sniffed the air, noting a spicy aroma of fresh-baked bread. It was another familiar thing in this strange place. Over at the dining table, Grandma passed around a platter of cardamom rolls with pearl sugar on top, just like the ones Mamma made at home.

"Come, sit, Joel," said Grandpa, calling him over.

"Would you boys like some *lingon dricka?*" asked Mamma. She poured sweet red juice into two glasses. "This was my favorite drink as a child."

Joel liked meeting these faraway relatives at last. In some ways they were just like he had imagined—old country with strange clothes and talk. But in other ways, they weren't strange at all. They were family. Grandpa and Mamma had the same long faces with sharp cheekbones and deep-set eyes. Grandma had a tiny mole by her mouth, same as Mamma.

Joel decided Grandma must love to cook, in spite of her blindness. Every part of her was round and soft, even her elbows. When she smiled, her eyes turned into little crescents.

"It's so good to have you back, Annali," said Grandpa.

Grandma nodded, reaching out for Mamma's hand. "It's like cotton around the heart to have you home with us."

Joel smiled at the expression remembering the many times he'd heard Mamma say it when she felt especially happy. Now he knew where it came from.

Mamma let her gaze wander around the room, as if trying to drink it all in. "It is like a dream to be here, Joel. You cannot know what coming home means to me, unless you have been away for as long as I have."

Deep in the pit of his stomach, Joel understood what coming home meant to his mother. Thirty-four years is a long time to not see your family. He tried to imagine what it would be like if he couldn't go back to Omaha, leaving behind family and friends. Never to sleep in his own room again. Never again go sledding with his friends down the hills in Hanscom Park. He didn't think he could stand it.

Axel tugged on his sleeve. "You get to stay in my room," he said. "It's up in the attic."

"Fine," said Joel. "I have an attic room at home, too."

Grandpa laughed. "When Axel heard you were coming, he begged your Uncle Johan to let him come up here for the summer. He's been counting the days."

"Do you like to fish?" asked Axel.

"Sure. At home I fish in the Missouri River."

"What a funny name!" Axel wrinkled his nose. "Miz-oo-ree."

"Sool-gordon! Smoe-land" Joel teased back, having some fun with the Swedish names Solgården and Småland.

"I can see you cousins will get along just fine," said Mamma. "You are both *'tokiga.'* Crazy!"

"Too-key-ga!" the two boys hooted at each other.

Mamma got up and wandered over to the bookshelf. Her hand caressed a carved wooden figure of a dancing couple.

"I remember when you made this, Pappa," she said. "I used to go out to your woodshed and watch you carve. Do you still do it?"

Grandpa laughed. "Ha! I have so many carvings in my shed I can barely fit in. You should come see them, Joel."

"Yes, I'd like that."

Grandma felt her way to the desk, opened a drawer, and took out a small rolled packet. She unrolled a dried ear of corn and showed it to Mamma. "Your brother Samuel sent this from his farm in Iowa."

"Everything grows big in America!" said Grandpa. "But now we grow corn here, too. We aren't as poor as you remember us, Annali."

"For that I am happy, Father. We were too many mouths to feed in the old days. Some of us had to leave so you could survive."

Grandma nodded. "Four of my babies left for America. One is in Heaven. You are the only one to come home."

"Many who left are moving back now," said Grandpa. "The government is making it easy to get land. New houses are going up everywhere. Our sawmill is busy every day."

Joel struggled to keep up with the conversation. There were so many new words flying back and forth. He wasn't sure he was getting it all. Then Grandpa asked a question he understood all too well.

"Have you ever thought of coming back to stay, Annali?"

Mamma smiled. "All the time, Father. All the time."

Joel couldn't believe his ears. Mamma had never ever said anything about wanting to move back to Sweden. Never. Not once. Could she really be thinking of moving back?

11
Troll Lessons

July 17, 1914

Mamma got her wish to see her parents again. It's a very strange place, Sweden. Everything is so old. I miss my bed at home. My bed here feels more like a feed crib. It's a wooden box with a hard mattress. At least I have a soft down comforter. But my back still aches from our long ride. I've finally met Grandma and Grandpa. They're nice. And old. Very old. It's good we came. All that Swede talk I heard at home is coming in handy. It's all around me now. New words, old words. I think Mamma is surprised how well I get along. Me too!

Joel put his journal down and listened to a soft patter of rain on the roof. His nose picked up the aroma of fresh coffee. He dressed, then stumbled downstairs.

"Good afternoon, *Mister* Peterson!" said Grandpa. He gestured toward the table. "Help yourself. On a full stomach sits a happy head, you know."

"Thanks." Joel stared at the pile of food in front of him. Could this be the same family Mamma had said never had enough? The family so poor the children were sent away to America so they wouldn't starve? He counted three kinds of bread, hard-boiled eggs, smoked fish, boiled potatoes, two cheeses, small meatballs, fresh milk, butter, jam, and fruit.

"Where is everyone?" he asked, making a sandwich of rye bread and cheese.

"Annali is helping Grandma dress her loom and Axel is waiting for you in the woodshed."

Joel laughed. "In America, going to the woodshed means you're in big trouble."

"Here too! But I think he just wants to show you my other little family!" Grandpa said. He wiggled his bushy eyebrows.

After breakfast, Joel followed him out the door. Outside, dark rain clouds scudded across the sky. The morning rain had left the yard a soggy mess. While Joel skipped around puddles, Grandpa lumbered right through them. They ducked into a small wooden shed where curls of wood shavings and sawdust littered the floor. Axel looked up from sawing a log, the scent of fresh-cut cedar filling the air.

"Come see my wood people," said Grandpa, nodding toward the shelves above his work bench.

Joel looked where he pointed and gasped. "Wow!" Dozens of carved figures stared back at him. He spotted a milkmaid and her cow, a fisherman, a hunter and his dog, a moose, several bears, ducks, pigs, and some odd creatures he couldn't identify.

"What are those?" he asked, pointing to a group of very ugly...he couldn't really call them "people."

Axel laughed. "Haven't you ever seen a troll?"

"No. Is that what they look like?" Joel reached for one and studied it. The face was mostly nose, with a dark bump on the very end.

"So you know something about trolls, do you?" asked Grandpa.

"My friend, Kari, told me a little on the ship. She said they were creatures that lived in the forests, rocks, or lakes. Not human. Not animal, either."

"*Ja,* that's so," said Grandpa.

"Have you ever seen one?" Joel asked.

Grandpa picked up a chunk of wood he'd been working on, studied it a moment, then started carving.

"Sometimes," he said, "when I'm going through the woods, the forest looks full of trolls. My eyes play tricks on me. Is that an old rock, or a fat troll? Is that a mossy log, or an sleeping troll?"

"But you haven't actually *seen* one?" Joel asked again.

Grandpa raised his eyebrows. "Ha! I even know them by name." He made a face and went back to his carving. "They are people who act like trolls. Greedy, selfish, and mean. I try to stay away from them."

Axel groaned. "I know a boy at school who's a real troll. He's always picking fights and getting me in trouble. Someday I'm going to punch him in the nose."

"Oh no, Axel," warned Grandpa. "Fighting only makes a troll stronger. You have to outsmart him. Figure out what his weak spot is. What is it that makes him act like a troll? Use that to trip him up."

Good advice, thought Joel. But how do you figure out what a person's weak spot was? He knew a few trolls back at his school, he'd like to trip.

Just then, the ting-a-ling of bells sounded in the yard. Axel ran out, but came back seconds later.

"It's a delivery wagon. Your trunks are here from the ship!"

"Hot dog!" shouted Joel in English. "I'm sick of wearing the same old clothes."

Together, he and Axel lugged the trunks across the yard and into the parlor, tracking mud and water everywhere.

"That was fast service!" said Mamma when she saw the trunks. "Someone must have packed for us on the ship."

Mamma carried piles of clothes upstairs, while Joel passed out the gifts they'd brought.

"This is the best toy," he said, helping Axel sort out the Erector set he'd brought for him. "We can build bridges, towers..."

A knock at the door made him look up.

"More trunks?"

But when Joel opened the door, a lanky gentleman stood there. He wasn't dressed in the rough clothes of a farmer. He looked like one of those fancy doormen at a hotel. Fine dark suit, new shoes and straw hat, and a sparkly stick pin in his tie.

"Good day," he said, taking off his hat. "I am looking for Annali Johansson. Is she at home?"

55

12
An Old Flame

Joel squinted up at the man. "Oh. You must mean my mother, Mrs. Peterson. And you are...?"

From behind him, Joel heard Mamma gasp.

"Gunnar Andersson! After all these years!"

"I would have known you anywhere," he said, sweeping into the room and taking Mamma's hand in his. "As beautiful as ever!"

Joel winced watching this strange man kiss his mother's hand. Who was he, anyway? Grayish blond hair fell casually across his forehead as he kept his cool, blue eyes fixed on Mamma. He might have been handsome except for a big wart on his nose.

"This is my son, Joel," said Mamma, beckoning Joel to come over and properly greet the visitor.

"Pleased to meet you, sir." Joel extended his hand and instantly regretted it. Herr Andersson gave him one of those finger-crunching handshakes that hurt for minutes afterwards.

"Your mother and I are old friends. In fact, she's the only woman to break my heart."

"Hush, Gunnar," said Mamma, waving him off. "You'll be putting ideas into the boy's head."

"But it's true! I wanted to marry her. But before I could get her to answer, she left for America."

"I was only twelve. Much too young to talk of marriage."

"Ah, but not too young to emigrate. So when I heard you had come home..." He finally turned and greeted Grandma. "Do you remember me, Fru Johansson?"

Grandma cocked her head. "You're Emil's boy, aren't you?"

He laughed. "Yes, that's true. But my parents have been dead for years now."

The man gave Joel the creeps. He reminded Joel of somebody, but he couldn't remember who.

"Do you still live around here?" Mamma asked.

The man rocked back on his heels, his hands in his pockets. "Here and there," he finally answered. "I travel quite a bit. But I'm home for a while." He gave the coins in his pocket a jingle. "I had hoped to buy the farm where I grew up. But the owner won't sell. I'll find another spot."

"A businessman," said Grandma. "With pockets full of money!"

Joel stifled a laugh, glancing over at Mamma. She had always said it was poor manners to comment on a person's money. But if you were Grandma's age, it seemed you could say anything you wanted, things others are thinking but don't dare speak.

Mamma ushered her guest over to the dining table. "Let me bring you some coffee. Then we can catch up on old times."

Before she disappeared into the kitchen, she whispered to Axel and Joel, "You boys go play, now. Let the grown-ups visit."

Axel nudged Joel as they headed out. "Who is that guy?"

"Some old boyfriend. I wonder what he wants?" Was he trying to show Mamma what a rich guy he was? Would she care?

Outside, Axel pulled Joel around the corner of the house. Quietly, they scrunched down under the window.

"What if they catch us?" Joel whispered.

"Shh!"

Laughter spilled out like tinkling glass.

"You've come a long way from the wild boy I knew so many years ago," Joel heard his mother say. "My father didn't think you'd amount to anything."

"Well, now see how wrong a person can be? Maybe you're thinking you should have married me after all?"

"Now don't you go flirting with me, Gunnar Andersson. I'm a happily married woman with a fine family."

"And where is the lucky husband?"

"Minding the store back in Omaha, thank you."

"A brave man to let his pretty wife out in the world alone. He'd better watch out. I might steal you away from him!"

Joel didn't like the way this visit was going at all. He was about to pop up and say so through the window when a dark shadow loomed over him.

"What's up?" asked Grandpa.

Axel fell back, startled. "Oh, you scared us!"

"Little pitchers also have ears, I see!"

"There's some fancy man visiting with Mamma. He's a real bragger," Joel muttered.

"What's his name?"

"Gunnar somebody."

"Not Gunnar Andersson?" asked Grandpa, a scowl on his face.

"That's him."

"Humph! Old Wart-nose! What's he doing back here?" He turned and headed into the house.

"Wart-nose?" Now Joel realized who the man reminded him of. One of Grandpa's trolls!

After a few moments, Joel heard voices saying goodbye. Good for Grandpa!

That night, before going to bed, Joel made a note in his journal:

Something is strange about the man who came to visit today. I don't like him. He has trouble looking me straight in the eye. And I don't like how he talks to Mamma. I'm sure glad Mamma didn't marry him. I wonder if she left for America all those years ago to get away from him? What would Pappa say? He'd probably tell me to keep an eye on this guy. And I will!

13
A Party for Mamma

July 19, 1914

"Aren't you awake yet?"

A flash of sunlight hit Joel's sleepy face as Axel yanked the blanket off the window. Summer nights here are not made for sleeping, thought Joel. Going to bed while the sun was still out made him feel like a little kid again. About midnight, the sun dipped below the horizon and there was an hour or two of dusk. Then by 2 A.M. it was as bright as midday again. So, just before going to bed, they covered the window to make it dark enough to sleep.

Axel tugged at the cocoon Joel had made of his quilts.

"Come on! Today's the party!"

Joel peeked at his watch and groaned. It was only 7:30. A pile of clothes sailed through the air, hitting his head.

"Quit it!" Joel stretched and gave his scalp a good scratch. "Did you say something about a party? With presents?"

"No presents. But lots of food."

"O.K. Sounds good."

About noon, friends, relatives and neighbors started arriving. Grandpa had set up two long tables in the yard. One for food, one for the guests. Mamma sent Axel and Joel out with bowls of sausages, red cabbage, herring, and boiled potatoes. So at least what Axel said about lots to eat was true. Joel's stomach was already growling.

One of the first to arrive was Axel's father, Uncle Johan, from Falkenberg. Axel pulled him over to meet Joel.

"I hope Axel hasn't been a bother to you, Joel. He doesn't have any little brother or sister to play with—yet," said Uncle Johan.

"Mamma couldn't come because she's waiting for a baby," explained Axel.

"We get along fine," said Joel. "I don't have a brother, either. Just one sister."

Soon the drive to the house filled with wagons and buggies. Relatives swarmed all over. Joel had a feeling he was related to everyone in Stentorp. At first, his Swedish cousins just stared at him, like he was some kind of two-headed cow. When they realized he could talk Swedish, they showered him with questions.

"Are you rich?"

"Do you know any Indians?"

"Have you ever dug for gold?"

Where do they get such ideas? thought Joel. Then he remembered his own fuzzy ideas about Sweden. He decided it would be more fun to go along with their notions than to say 'no.'

"Rich? I suppose so. With all the gold my Pappa found in the backyard, we built a new house ten stories high with crystal lights in every room."

"Ooooh," the cousins sighed.

"As for Indians," continued Joel, "they live out on the prairie. I usually spend my summers with them learning to ride bareback on horses."

"Can you shoot an arrow?" one cousin asked.

"Oh sure. Everybody can do that!"

The cousins seemed very impressed.

Mamma flitted to all the visitors, greeting them with hugs and kisses. She had dressed up in a colorful striped skirt, a flowered scarf, and a white blouse with huge puffy sleeves. She had even changed her hair from a tight bun to a long braid down her back. Joel didn't know much about ladies' clothes, but he could tell these changes made her feel different today. She wasn't quite so...Mother. More like a schoolgirl. At home, she rarely laughed. Today, she was all smiles and giggles. He hardly knew her.

Joel frowned when he spotted Gunnar Andersson among the guests. Mamma hurried over to greet him. He bowed, handing her a bouquet of flowers. Joel noticed after a while that the man never left her side, following her everywhere, as if the party were for his homecoming, too.

"Come on, Axel. Let's go see what he's up to."

The boys scurried over to the table just as Mamma and Gunnar sat down.

"Hello again, Herr Andersson. I'm not sure you remember me. I'm Joel Peterson."

"Ah, yes! The young Swede comes back to see the homeland!" He doffed his hat, a gold tooth flashing with his smile.

"But I'm not a Swede, I'm an Ameri— "

Mamma gave Joel one of those 'children-should-be-seen-and-not-heard' looks.

"You must pardon my son," she said to Gunnar. "I'm afraid American boys are a lot more outspoken than Swedish boys." She nodded toward Axel, smiling sweetly at him.

"No harm in that," said Gunnar. "I met a number of spunky young men in my travels around America."

"Do tell!" said Mamma, her eyes wide. "What brought you over there?"

"Business. Investments. I spend a few months every year traveling around, meeting people." He pulled out a fat cigar, lit it and sent smelly puffs of smoke in Joel's direction. "But now I'm looking to settle down. Buy some land, build a nice manor house."

"You don't have a home in the States?"

"Absolutely not. I find the place crawling with crime. Gets worse every year."

Mamma nodded. "My brothers were cheated many times when they first arrived. And by their own countrymen, too!"

Gunnar coughed, he eyes shifting to the ground. "Ah yes, a real shame. The strong take advantage of the weak. But lots of those emigrants are getting wise. They're moving back to Sweden now. They realize this is where home really is." He leaned close to Mamma and said, almost in a whisper, "Is that why you've come home, Annali?"

Mamma shook her head. "I've lived most of my life on the American prairie. And I've missed my homeland and my family. But I'm an American now. So is my husband."

Gunnar flicked an ash from his cigar. "Yes, I see. But what if there was a war? What if Sweden and the U.S. ended up on opposite sides? How would you feel then?"

Mamma turned and faced him, startled. "War? Who said anything about war?"

"I hear rumors," said Gunnar. "Tempers are short all over Europe this summer."

Mamma dismissed him with a wave of her hand. "I don't listen to rumors. All I know is that it's grand to be home again one more time in life."

Gunnar grinned, placing his hand on hers. "But, don't you see? It doesn't have to be for just one time! Why not come back here where you belong? Doesn't your husband long for the homeland?"

"No!" shouted Joel, jumping up.

They both turned and stared at him. Bad manners or not, he had to say something.

"Pappa is happy in Omaha. He has a good business there and wants me to work for him." Joel took a deep breath, trying to control his anger. "It's fine to come for a visit. But we *will* go back to America!" He turned and hurried back to the house before he said anything else. That man made his skin itch. Why won't he leave Mamma alone? Why was he trying to talk her into moving back?

He had almost reached the door when he felt someone tug at his sleeve.

"Slow down, son," said a skinny man in a dark frock coat.

It was the local schoolmaster. He reminded Joel of Ichabod Crane, the teacher in Washington Irving's story "The Legend of Sleepy Hollow." Like Ichabod, Herr Ullman was tall and lanky, with knobby hands, hollowed cheeks, and a pointy Adam's apple that bobbled as he spoke. Just knowing that a teacher had him by the arm was enough to make Joel get control of himself. He wondered if the schoolmaster was going to take out a ruler and smack his knuckles for being so rude just now. But instead, he motioned for the two of them to sit on the stoop.

"Um...What can I do for you, Herr Ullman?" Joel muttered.

"This trip to the old homeland is more for your mother, isn't it?"

"Yes...she needed to see her family. But I'm glad to meet my grandparents."

Mr. Ullman smiled, looking across the yard at the guests. "But it must get rather dull, all this visiting with people you don't know."

Joel shrugged, not quite sure how he should answer.

"Tell you what. I've arranged to take a small group of boys, all about your age, on a short trip to the continent. We'll be gone about ten days, visiting museums, some of the great German castles. Would you like to come along?"

Joel looked up, surprised. "Oh, yes. Absolutely! But, I'd have to ask my mother."

"I took the liberty of speaking to her about it already. She agrees it would be very educational for you. But of course, it's entirely up to you."

Joel glanced over at the people at the tables. Mamma seemed to be apologizing to everyone. His burst of anger had sent waves of heat rolling up his back, tingling his hair. So many ideas pulled tug-of-war in his head. If I stayed here I could keep an eye on that Gunnar guy, he reasoned. But a trip to Germany....wow! The lure of travel and new places was too much to pass up. He stood and shook hands with the schoolmaster, adding a polite bow from the waist.

"I'd be happy to join your group. Thank you for asking me."

"Excellent. I'll make all the arrangements. We leave in two weeks," said Herr Ullman. Then he strode off to join the others.

Later that night, Joel hunched over the kerosene lamp writing in his journal:

Good and bad at the party today. Old Wart-nose showed up. I don't like him filling Mamma's head with stupid ideas about moving back to Sweden. He's scaring her, too, with crazy ideas about war. Whose side would we be on? America's, of course! What a question! I knew Mamma was disappointed with me. Tonight, before coming to bed, I brought her some wildflowers. I told her I was sorry for losing my temper. She forgave me. She had such a good time, she couldn't stay mad. Then she asked if Mr. Ullman had talked to me. She smiled when I told her I'd decided to go along on the tour. I hope I made the right decision.

14
A Letter From a Girl

July 20, 1914

The next morning dawned warm and sunny. Joel sat on a rock outside the house, picking his way through a newspaper article. It was the second time he'd seen his name in a paper recently.

EMIGRANT RETURNS IN STYLE
Thirty-four years after Annali Johansson left for the Great Land to the west, Solgården celebrates her return with a gathering of friends and family. Fru Annali Johansson Peterson and her son, Joel, reside in Omaha, Nebraska, where Herr Alfred Peterson owns a prosperous tailoring business. The visitors will stay in Småland for one month before touring the Continent. Welcome back!

Joel looked up as Mamma marched out with one of Grandma's rag rugs folded her arms. She threw it

68

over a clothes line and started whacking it with a broom, sending great puffs of dust into the air. Joel smiled. The stylish emigrant returns to beat rugs. She works as hard here as at home, he thought. Remembering he had chores to do, too, he headed for the barn to help.

While Grandpa carried loads of manure and straw out to the dump pile, Joel mucked out the stalls. It was smelly work so he let his mind wander over the events of the past few days. After a while, Grandpa caught him leaning on his rake and staring into space.

"You'll get no work done daydreaming, Joel!"

"I was thinking about that man."

"What man?"

"Herr Andersson. He stuck to Mamma yesterday like a bee in jam."

"He is a pest!" Grandpa snorted. He started shoveling more manure into his wheelbarrow.

"You never liked him, did you? Even long ago?"

"He was a no-good sneak," answered Grandpa in disgust. "He'd be telling Annali he wanted to marry her, and then I'd see him walking arm in arm with some other young lady."

"But that was a long time ago. Is he still a sneak?"

Grandpa nodded. "I've heard from some of my friends with relatives in America that he cheated them on land deals over there."

So that's what kind of "business" he was in! thought Joel. No wonder he doesn't talk about where he's been and what he's done.

"Why hasn't he been arrested?"

"Hasn't been caught, I guess. Maybe you should find out why he left America. Maybe they kicked him out!" Grandpa stood up and wiggled his bushy eyebrows, obviously relishing the thought of Gunnar in trouble.

Joel thrust his rake at the pile of straw at the back of Pelle's stall. The more he thought about that man, the more he felt his anger rise. If Mamma knew the truth about him, he wouldn't dare come show his warty nose around here again! Thinking of him as a troll made Joel remember something Grandpa had said. *Figure out what it is that makes him act like a troll. Then use that to trip him up.*

Joel put the rake aside and wandered out into the yard, deep in thought. He almost walked smack into Axel, who was sopping wet from giving Pelle a bath.

"Good idea, cousin. You both needed a bath!"

"Ha, ha," sneered Axel. He pulled off his blue cap and took out a small envelope he had tucked inside, waving it over his head. "Maybe I won't give this to you then. It's from a *girl*."

Joel snatched the letter from him. Sure enough, the return address read "Kari Berg, Café Bryggan, Christiania." He tore it open and read:

> *July 17, 1914*
> *Christiania*

Dear Joel,

Greetings from Norway! I was so happy to get the message you left for me. I didn't know what to think when I didn't see you at the pier. I was afraid you didn't want to see me anymore.

I'm working ten hours a day in Uncle's restaurant. I have my own small room upstairs, but it's right over the kitchen, so it always smells like fish. Uncle Ivar is so different from my parents. Last night he cursed at me for dropping some dishes. Everyone in the restaurant heard him. Later, he tried to make up with a big, slobbery kiss. I try to stay away from him, but it is hard in this small place. I don't know how long I can stay with him. But where else can I go?

Thank you for helping me on the ship. It was a hard time then.

Please, if you want to, write back to me. You are the only friend I have over here. I'm so homesick. But where is home? It is not in America and it is not here, either. Write soon.

Your friend from the ship,
Kari Berg

Joel clenched his fists tight as he finished her letter. It wasn't fair! Kari deserved better than an uncle who took advantage of her, who treated her more like a servant than a niece. If only she had come with them to Sweden....

"Joel! We could use some extra hands in here," Mamma called from the house.

"Coming!" Joel hurried in to see what was the matter, taking Kari's letter with him.

Mamma sat on the bench at Grandma's old wooden loom, patiently threading strands of yarn through strings harnessed in the center. As she tied off a group of threads, she nodded toward the kitchen.

71

"Grandma had a small accident just now. Can you get a mop and help her clean up? I can't stop this job or I'll forget the pattern she wanted."

"Uh...sure. When you get a chance, would you read this?" He placed Kari's letter on the bench.

In the kitchen, Grandma struggled to move a big copper tub. Soapy water slopped all over the floor.

"Here, Grandma, let me do that."

"Move it to the back door, Joel, then dump it."

He shoved the tub across the floor, taking care not to slip in the soapy water. At the door, he heaved it over, sending water down the steps to the yard.

"*Tack så mycket!*" said Grandma, sinking into a chair. "This didn't used to be so hard." Her wrinkled hand brushed wispy gray hairs from her face.

"Were you trying to wash the floor?"

"No. That was laundry water. But I guess we'll wash it now!"

"I'll do it. You sit." Joel grabbed a mop and began swishing it across the floor. By the time the job was done, Mamma stood in the doorway holding Kari's letter.

"Poor girl," she said. "It reminds me of when I first went to America. My Aunt Lena was supposed to send me to school. Instead, I became her housemaid. Until I ran away."

"Where did you go?" Joel asked.

"To Omaha. I called on the minister's family. They took me in and I finally did get to go to school."

Joel leaned on the mop, thinking. He had an idea, but he wasn't sure Mamma would agree. "Kari doesn't have anyone else," he said. "Just us."

Mamma folded her arms, studying him. "What are you saying? Kari is not our responsibility."

"No, but..." He glanced around at the wet floor. "She could be a lot of help around here." Joel walked over and put his arm around Grandma's small shoulders. "Tell us, *Mormor,* how do you set up your loom when Mamma's not here?"

Grandma groaned and shook her head, chuckling to herself. "Elof tries to help, but his big hands are no good with fine threads. I have to wait until a neighbor comes by to help me."

Joel gave her shoulder a pat. "My friend is a hard worker. And a nice girl. She'd be good for you." He didn't want to push, but he thought this might be the only way out for Kari.

Slowly, the tired wrinkles in Grandma's face melted with her smile. "Annali, this is a smart boy you have. If he thinks so much of this girl, then she must be very special. It would almost be like having you near me again!"

Joel wanted to run out in the yard and turn somersaults. Instead, he gave Grandma a kiss on the cheek, then bounded up the stairs to write a letter back to Kari.

15
Trollbacken

July 25, 1914

Long summer days dragged on, the skies drizzling rain on and off. Mamma and Grandma spent hours knitting and talking, baking and talking, and talking some more. Now and then, Mamma would mention Joel's name, bragging about him. She didn't seem to realize how much more Swede talk he understood now. Joel decided not to let on. More fun to listen in that way!

At last the rain let up and Grandpa suggested a fishing trip to a nearby lake. Axel found an extra pole and the three of them headed down the road. They passed a few farms, then turned off onto a well-worn trail through a rocky field. In the center, Joel noticed an old chimney sticking up through the ruins.

"What's that?" he asked.

"Trollbacken," answered Grandpa.

"It looks like a spook house," said Axel.

It didn't look like much of a house at all to Joel—just a pile of rocks half hidden by weeds and moss-covered black logs.

Over the hill, they came to a shimmering lake tucked in among pine and birch trees. Grandpa hauled out an old gray rowboat he had hidden in the brush. He tipped it over, dumping out the rainwater that had collected in the bottom.

"Hop in, boys," he said.

Joel stared at the damp ribs and the worn bench. He doubted it would even float.

"Go on. It won't sink," said Axel, as if reading his mind.

The little boat wobbled and sloshed as they climbed in, Axel and Joel at the rear, Grandpa in the center. Grandpa stuck his oar into the bank and pushed off. With strong, even strokes, he rowed them out to the center of the lake.

After baiting their hooks, they sat quietly, shooing away flies and waiting for a bite. For once, Axel wasn't chattering. But every now and then, Grandpa would lean near the water and whisper, *"Kom, kom, lilla fisk. Bit i masken, så blir du frisk."*

Come, come, little fish. Bite the worm, it's good for you.

Joel checked his line, his thoughts wandering back to the ruin they'd passed.

"Grandpa, tell me about that spook house."

Axel looked up, his eyes sparkling. "I want to hear, too."

Grandpa pulled out his pipe, stuffed some tobacco in the bowl and lit it. Curls of wispy smoke rose into the air.

"It all began when a blacksmith from another town decided to move here with his young wife. In those days, we had to go to Vetlanda for a blacksmith. So everyone was happy when they showed up. He looked to buy some land and decided on this place, Trollbacken. It had a nice hill in the middle and the blacksmith figured that would be a good spot for his house and shop. Trollbacken had been in our family for years but never cultivated. My father thought they would build on the low land. When he heard they were going to build on the hill, he tried to warn them.

'Don't do it!' he said. 'There's little folk living under that hill. They don't like it when Christian folk move in on top of them.'"

"But the blacksmith built there anyway?" Joel asked.

"*Ja,* that he did," said Grandpa. "He laughed at the warning.

"'I don't believe in fairy tales, old man!' he said. And so the man and his wife started to build. Every day it seemed they lost a tool or a piece of lumber. The couple argued, accusing each other of being careless with things. Once, after the man had spent all day building the chimney to the forge, the stones he had used tumbled down in a heap the next day.

"The neighbors understood what was going on. 'It's the little folk, the small trolls under the hill that are causing your troubles. Go build your smithy somewhere else. You'll be better off.'

"The two newcomers ignored them. In spite of all the delays, they finally got their house and smithy built."

"So why is it gone now?" asked Axel.

"Well, there's more to the story," said Grandpa, puffing on his pipe. "One night, as they were getting ready for bed, they heard clanging noises from outside. The man lit a lantern and went out to see what it was. He was shocked to see all his hammers, nails, iron rods, buckets, and pliers scattered about the yard.

'We're not leaving!' the man shouted into the darkness.

'Ooooo-hooo!' came the reply.

'It's only an owl,' said the man's wife.

'Ooooo-hooo!' once again.

"The blacksmith went about his business taking care of people's horses and wagons. He kept the forge burning night and day. His customers asked how it was going, and to every one he replied, 'Just fine, thank you.'

"One day, the blacksmith was asked to come to a farm many miles away. It meant he'd have to stay the night.

'Now don't you worry,' he told his wife. 'You'll be just fine while I'm away.'

"But the man's wife wasn't so sure. That night she locked all the doors and windows and pulled the curtains tightly closed. Whatever went on outside would be no concern of hers.

"Before going to bed, she decided to have one more cup of coffee. As she lifted her kettle from the

77

hearth, something snatched it out of her hand and sent it clattering across the floor.

"She peered into the dark shadows of her kitchen and saw a hairy troll staring back at her. He was no bigger than a cat, with a long, crooked nose. Clumps of mossy hair sprouted between the warts covering his body.

'What do you want?' the woman asked.

'Gold and silver and copper,' the troll answered.

'You've come to the wrong house, then. The only gold here is my wedding ring, and you're not getting that!'

'Gold and silver and copper. Gold and silver and copper,' said the troll over and over. He danced around the room, knocking pots and pans and dishes to the floor.

'Get out of my house!' yelled the woman. But in the next moment, it was she who was out of the house, standing barefoot in the yard. She ran down the road and did not stop until she came to the church. There, she huddled in a cold corner until the pastor found her in the morning.

"All through the night, a fire raged through the blacksmith's house and forge. The neighbors tried in vain to put out the stubborn flames of gold, silver, and copper.

"The blacksmith returned home to find his house in ruins and his wife half crazy. He gave back the land, moved away to another town and was never seen again.

"Some people say when the moon is full, they have seen the little trolls dancing in the ruins on the hill.

And if you listen carefully, you can still hear them singing, 'Gold and silver and copper' all night long."

The little rowboat rocked on the water. Off in the woods a bird screeched.

"Could be a troll," whispered Axel.

Grandpa winked at him. "Could be!"

Joel shook himself out of the story's trance. There's no such thing as trolls, he thought. Just then, a tug on his line scared him so, he almost fell in the water. But instead of a troll, he reeled in a huge pike.

"Won't Mamma be surprised to see this!"

But when they got home, Joel was the one who got a surprise.

16
A Party for Joel

July 25, 1914

"When—how—did you get here?" The words tumbled out of Joel's mouth as he stared at Kari in disbelief. He wanted to shake her hand in welcome, but his own hands were full of fishing gear.

Kari grinned at him. "I arrived at noon. You were already gone fishing," she said.

"I can't believe you're really here!"

"But you arranged it all! When I got your letter saying there was a job for me here, I told Uncle I was leaving. He didn't understand why. I used the money from the cigar box to get my ticket. And here I am!"

Mamma put her arm around Kari's shoulder, giving her a motherly pat. "You picked a good time to come. Tomorrow is Joel's birthday. But since you are here now, maybe we can celebrate tonight." She checked on his reaction. "Is that all right with you, Joel?"

"Yes. Fine. Yes," he stammered. He felt like a bum with grimy hands and clothes. "I guess I'd better clean up." He shoved his rod and fish at Axel. "Here. You take these."

Arms full, Axel lumbered out into the yard. But not before he whispered to Joel, "Lover-boy!"

Since there was no extra room in the house, Joel helped Grandpa fix up a temporary place for Kari in the barn. Next to the feed room was another small room where hired help once stayed. It had just enough room for a narrow bed, a table, and a wooden chair.

"It's only for a short while," he explained. "Until Mamma, Axel, and I leave. Then you can have the room in the attic."

Kari plopped her bags down on the bed. "This will be just fine! Much better than my smelly room over the kitchen."

That night after dinner, Mamma brought in a cake layered with whipped cream and strawberries. They made Joel stand up as Grandpa led everyone in singing,

Ja, må han leva, Ja, må han leva,
Ja, må han leva uti hundrade år!

It was the same song they always sang back home in Omaha. "Yes, may he live a hundred years. Yes, for sure he will live a hundred years!" Then everybody cheered, *Hurra! Hurra! Hurra!* Now he was finally thirteen. At home Pappa would have teased him that he was starting his fourteenth year.

For presents, he got a blue knit sweater from Mamma. Grandma gave him a small rug with scraps woven in from everyone's old clothes.

"Thank you, Grandma!" Joel said. "I will think of all of you each time I see it."

"And who will you think of when you see this?" asked Grandpa, handing him a hand-carved troll. It had dry moss for hair, a back covered with rabbit fur, and a long fat nose with a peppercorn glued on the end.

"You-know-who!" said Joel with a laugh.

Axel added some troll children made of pine cones.

"I didn't know it was your birthday, Joel," said Kari. "So I don't have anything for you. Except best wishes!"

"But you are my gift," he blurted out, his face growing warm. "I mean... it's so nice you're here." He didn't care if he blushed. It was true. Having Kari in Sweden was the best gift of all.

At eight o'clock, one party guest arrived that Joel wasn't so pleased to see. Gunnar Andersson marched in, puffing on a cigar, as usual. Before Joel could stop him, Gunnar gave him another finger-crunching handshake. But this time he left behind a crumpled five-dollar bill.

"To spend when you are back in America!" he hooted, slapping Joel on the back. Then, turning toward Mamma he added, "Unless we can convince you to stay."

Grandma reached out for Mamma's hand. "Oh, that would be lovely. But think of poor Alfred. He must be so lonesome."

Mamma smiled, looking down at her hands. "Yes, I expect he is."

Joel pocketed the five dollars, mumbling a "Thank you." But Gunnar wasn't paying attention to him anymore. He was staring at Kari as if trying to place her.

"I see you have made a friend, Joel," he said. "A pretty Swedish friend."

"American, actually," said Kari. "Joel and I met on the ship."

Gunnar tugged at his mustache, his eyes fixed on Kari. "Hm. A young American lady who speaks Swedish like a Norwegian. Interesting."

Mamma answered for her. "Soon our Kari will sound like a real Småland girl."

Joel wanted to change the subject. "Grandpa, tell everyone about all the fish we caught today at the lake."

"Ach! They were too big to take home. We threw them back." Grandpa wiggled his eyebrows again, this time at Kari. She grinned at his big lie.

Gunnar's eyes lit up. "I've been hoping to buy some land with a lake. I've looked at several places. But nothing fits what I want."

"Isn't there some old legend or story about the land around that lake, Father?" asked Mamma.

Grandpa shrugged. "Could be. Don't quite remember." He looked over at Axel and Joel and winked.

As Mamma passed the cake around for second helpings, Kari leaned over to Joel and whispered in his ear. "Could you show me where the outhouse is?"

"Sure. Come on," he said.

Outside, Kari stopped him. "I didn't really need to find the outhouse. I wanted to talk to you. Away from him."

"Away from who?"

"That man. The one who gave you the five dollars. I've seen him before."

"You have? Where?"

"He came into Café Bryggan a couple of times. Each time he got a card game going."

"He's a gambler?"

"Remember on the ship those signs warning the passengers about card sharks?" asked Kari. "Well, one of them is sitting in your parlor right now! And that's not all. The last time he was in, a fight broke out. Something about swindling people over land in America."

So Grandpa had been right about Gunnar Andersson! Joel didn't think Mamma knew. She wouldn't tolerate a gambler and a swindler. She hated people like that who preyed on the unsuspecting, cheating them out of their hard-earned savings. Joel wanted to rush in and let her know.

"I've got to say something, Mamma should know," he huffed, heading for the house.

"Wait!" Kari grabbed his arm. "He'd just deny it. You don't have any proof. And if you say I told you, he could make things hard on me here. Wait until the time is right."

Joel paused, gritting his teeth. He knew Kari was right. "That time better come soon. I may not be able to wait. And in a few days I'm leaving for Germany."

"But I just got here."

"It's only for ten days. The local schoolmaster invited me. It was all decided before I even wrote to you. Besides, you'll be so busy helping Grandma and getting used to things here, you won't even notice I'm gone."

Kari brushed her hand against his. "That's a lie and you know it, Joel Peterson!"

Joel was glad it was dusky out so Kari couldn't see him blush.

17
Off to the Continent

July 30, 1914

Dear Uncle Karl,

I'm on my way to Germany! Our train left Vetlanda this morning, heading south for "the continent." That's what they call going across to the main European lands. The Continent. Sounds like another world but it's only a few miles across the water from Sweden.

The schoolmaster and his son Jakob, who is twelve, picked me up at 8 A.M. Our trip will take all day and night. We met our other travel chums at the Vetlanda train depot. Karl-Johan and Ragnar are fourteen and fifteen. I've never seen hair as white as theirs. It makes the pink of their cheeks even brighter. They're also as skinny as farm scarecrows. Jakob calls them "Kalle" and "Ragge." They both speak German and a little English and have promised to translate for me as we go.

I feel like I'm on my first assignment as a reporter. You'd be proud of me, Uncle Karl! I'll be your eyes and ears and take lots of notes.

Joel stared out the window as the southern town of Trelleborg came into view. The trip had been rather boring so far, a lot of farms and whitewashed buildings with red-tiled roofs. To break the monotony, the boys had explored the train from end to end. Jakob, the tallest of the group, kept bumping his head in the narrow doorways between the cars.

"My father says I will soon be taller than he is," Jakob grumbled, rubbing his forehead. "If that's true, I'll have to spend my whole life bent over so I don't get headaches from hitting things."

"Don't complain. You'll always have the best view of things in a crowd," said Kalle.

"Yeah, if we get lost, we'll just look for the Tower of Jakob," teased Ragge.

Before going back to their seats, they bought candy and fruit from a vendor. Their sandwiches brought from home were long gone and the quick supper between trains seemed like hours ago to Joel. He pulled out Pappa's silver watch. It was almost midnight. He hoped the ferry had food.

Outside the window, the sky had turned dusky. The buildings slipped by slower as the train crawled into town, jerking and screeching as it switched tracks. Finally, it lurched to a stop at the ferry docks.

"Outside, gentlemen," ordered Herr Ullman, leading his troop out onto the platform.

"Come on," urged Kalle, "Let's go watch them put the train on the ferry." The boys scrambled up to a staircase where they could watch the procedure. The cool, salty sea breeze felt refreshing after the stuffy train.

Rail cars rumbled back and forth on the tracks as they were uncoupled, backed up, and realigned into the belly of the huge ferry boat. Whistles screamed, metal clanged against metal, and men shouted orders to each other. Down by the water, a flurry of seagulls swooped in circles, finding bits of food floating in the water.

"Won't it sink?" Joel shouted over the noise.

"Nah!" Ragge yelled back. "We've crossed before like this."

Down below they saw Herr Ullman waving for them to come. They hurried to join him so they could board the ferry and find places up front. By the time the train and people were all loaded, the short summer night had passed and the pale dawn of a new day glowed on the horizon.

At 3 A.M. the ferry arrived at the German port of Sassnitz. They switched to a German train and settled in for the final leg to Berlin. After staying up all night, Joel fought to stay awake and see the countryside. But the clackity-clack of the rail and the rhythmic swaying of the cars soon lulled him to sleep. The next thing he knew, Jakob was poking him saying,

"We're here!"

Joel peered out the window as the train entered the smoky Berlin rail terminal.

As he stepped out on the platform, crowds of people swarmed around him. Where were they all going? he wondered. A noisy buzz echoed through the cavernous terminal. Anxious faces flashed past him as strange sounds of German chatter filled the air. Joel spotted a boy selling newspapers. He reached in his pocket for coins to buy one, but all he had was Swedish money.

Seeing the problem, Herr Ullman led them all up to an exchange window where they could get some German marks. With his money exchanged, Joel ran back and bought a paper. But when he looked at the front page, he scowled. German! He couldn't even read the headlines. He thrust the paper at Kalle and Ragge.

"What does it say?"

"Something about trouble between Germany and Russia. There was an assassination last June in Serbia.....and now talk of war!" read Kalle, his eyes wide.

Ragge pointed to another article. "Hey, this is interesting. The Tsar of Russia is cousin to the German Kaiser Wilhelm. Since they're cousins, they won't go to war, will they?"

"Who knows. But something's up, I can feel it!" said Joel as he tucked the paper under his arm. The hair on his neck prickled. It reminded him of how he felt in the moments before the spring tornado hit last year. As the sky darkened, restless birds had swooped in dizzy circles around the neighborhood. One even smacked into the parlor window, breaking its neck in the hurry to find shelter. Joel willed himself to stay alert, eyes and ears open.

18
The Great War Begins

August 1-2, 1914

Dear Uncle Karl,

Our first day in Berlin was great. We were all tired but we didn't want to miss anything. After we got settled in our hotel, we spent the day exploring Tiergarten Park and the zoo. The city is full of old stone buildings, streaked with dark soot. Omaha will seem so new and fresh when I get back. But the streets here are lined with trees and the River Spee runs right through the city. I'm constantly hungry because the air is full of great food smells—fresh bread, sausages, onions. Yum. Every corner has a bakery with tons of sweets. Kalle, Ragge, and Jakob each ate six pastries! I won't admit my score.

We are as tired as dogs. Early to bed, early to rise. Tomorrow we visit the museums and maybe the royal palace!

Herr Ullman rousted the boys early, assembling everyone in the hotel lobby to plan the day.

"If we time it right, we can get in on a tour of the palace by noon. Museums will come later. Keep an eye on each other and don't stray. I've never seen Berlin so crowded. Your parents would not be pleased if I lost any of you!"

The energy Joel had sensed the day before at the train station was still buzzing today. On one corner. he noticed a group of men huddled in front of a newspaper kiosk, reading the latest edition of the paper and shouting about something.

Herr Ullman tried to ignore the nervousness all around, giving a running talk about the government of today and kings of the past. Every few steps Joel would stop to make notes in his journal. Then he'd have to run to catch up. More than once, Herr Ullman looked annoyed with him.

"Stay together everyone! Now as I was saying..."

The group continued through town, stopping now and then as Herr Ullman explained the history of some building or statue. A huge clock outside a jewelry store caught Joel's attention. He stopped a moment to check the time on his watch. As he tucked the watch back in his pocket, he spied a display of music boxes in the store window. Up ahead, Herr Ullman was still lecturing. Joel figured he had enough time to duck into the store and ask about a music box. Maybe this was something he could bring Kari as a gift.

"May I see that small one, please," he asked in English, pointing to a wooden box with a flower carved on the lid.

"Of course, sir," the clerk answered in English.

When Joel opened it, a happy waltz tune filled the air. "Nice. What is the name of this song?"

"'*Uber den Wellen*.' In English, 'Over the Waves'."

Joel smiled. It was perfect! Every time Kari heard this song, she would remember how they met on the ship. He paid for the music box and had the clerk wrap it carefully.

But when he came out again on the street, his group was nowhere in sight. He felt his chest tighten, thinking how angry Herr Ullman would be with him for lagging behind. Now, hundreds of people flowed down the sidewalks, spilling over into the street. Bodies brushed by him, shoving him along, like a cork caught in a swift-moving current. Everyone seemed to be heading in the same direction. He had no choice but to follow and hope he could find his group up ahead.

Clerks bustled out of shops, locked the doors, and joined the masses. A group of students, marching with arms locked together, were blocking traffic in the street. The song they were singing sounded powerful and patriotic. He wondered what it was about.

After being swept along for a few blocks, Joel realized everyone had gathered on the plaza outside the Kaiser's palace. He was lost in an ocean of strangers who cheered, clapped their hands in unison, and sang powerful-sounding songs. A lady rushed up to a soldier and stuck a small bouquet of flowers on his pointed helmet. Joel stood on tiptoe, craning his neck as he scanned the crowd for familiar faces. He edged around to different sections

until finally he spotted The Tower of Jakob, the
lanky schoolmaster and two white-haired boys.

"Here you are!" said Jakob. "Father was frantic!"

"Where were you?" asked Kalle.

"Right back there, with a few thousand other
people!" said Joel, laughing nervously. "Anybody
know what's going on? Is it a holiday?"

A roar erupted from the crowd. Horns tooted.
People hugged each other and waved handkerchiefs
in the air. Suddenly, the crowd started singing the
German national anthem.

Ragge tapped Joel's arm. "It's war! I just heard
the guard make an announcement to the crowd.
Germany has declared war on Russia!"

War! A rush of excitement ran up his spine as his
thoughts raced. You asked for it, Joel. You wanted to
be where the action was and now you are!

He stood there, dazed by all the emotion and
excitement swirling around him. It felt odd, too, like
he and his friends were uninvited guests at someone
else's party. But they couldn't cheer or sing along or
feel happy about going to war.

Herr Ullman waved his arms, motioning for them
to follow. Moving against the flow of people wasn't
easy as they fought their way back toward the hotel.
Joel hugged his wrapped package close, making sure
he didn't drop it or lose it. He felt especially glad he
had already bought the gift. Each shop they passed
was now closed tight.

19
The Mad Dash Back

Sunday August 2, 1914

WAR!!! I'm right in the middle of things, Uncle Karl. It's chaos. Hardly time to write. We're packed and ready to head back to Sweden. Met a fellow Swede this morning coming from Paris. Warned us to get out of Germany fast. Fighting has started on the German-French borders. The banks are closed, the hotel clerk won't take our money. The Swedish man exchanged money with us so we could pay the bill. Now to the train depot with hopes we can catch a ride back to Sassnitz. What a mess! Wish I could stay and see what happens. Herr Ullman is calling us....

The taxi could only get within a few blocks of the station. Joel and the others sprinted the rest of the way, joining the mob around the ticket booths. Thanks to their Swedish friend at the hotel, Herr

Ullman had just enough German marks to purchase tickets for all of them. Other travelers weren't so lucky and shoved wads of foreign money at him, begging to buy the tickets. He waved them away and ushered the boys down to the rail platforms.

Inside, it was noisy bedlam. Whistles screeched, loudspeakers crackled with unintelligible announcements, people shouted in a dozen languages, small children cried, and a pair of dogs tied to a post barked at everything. Fighting for every step, Joel and the rest made their way to Platform 12, where their train for Sassnitz waited. So many faces peered out from the windows, Joel wondered if there could be any room left for them. The conductor checked their tickets, urging them to hurry aboard.

Every seat was taken, sometimes with three or four squeezed into seats meant for two. The boys edged down the aisle, finally realizing that standing up was their only option. Several passengers shoved open the windows, letting in a little fresh air. With so many sweaty bodies, crying babies, and hot air, for a moment Joel was afraid he'd throw up and make things even worse.

Another loud whistle screamed. Steam hissed from underneath the train, clouding those left on the platform. Slowly, the train eased out of the station.

His energy spent, Joel slumped down on his carpet bag crammed between his feet. This would be his spot for the next six hours. His whole body felt weak and his head pounded. Maybe being in the center of the action wasn't so great after all, he thought.

At the ferry boat, they were caught up in more chaos. German soldiers prodded the crowd with their rifles, trying to keep order. Russian soldiers glared back at them as they pushed their way onto the ferry to Russia. All along the waterfront, Joel saw "war boats" lined up, ready to go to work—light cruisers, small troop carriers, and a strange low vessel he'd never seen before.

"A U-boat," cried Jakob, pointing at the same strange boat.

"*Unterseeboot*," Ragge explained. "Undersea boat, a submarine."

Hundreds packed the ferry boat for Trelleborg. People huddled on benches, sprawled on the decks, small children curled up under benches and tables. A steady rain began, soaking everyone who wasn't under some kind of cover. Joel and the boys decided the best place to be was in the food line. After two hours, they finally got some small sandwiches and cups of hot tea. Herr Ullman was one of the lucky ones, having found a bench, and was sound asleep, his head resting on another sleeping passenger.

At 6 A.M. and a long train ride later, Herr Ullman's hired buggy pulled into Solgården. Mamma and Kari came rushing out the door as Joel grabbed his bag and jumped down.

Mamma squeezed him tight. "I have been worried sick," she sobbed.

Over her shoulder he saw Kari, a shawl hastily thrown around her nightdress. He grinned at her. She looked great, even with her hair messy from sleep.

"We got news of the war last night," said Kari, "from the pastor. He rode all over the village and to all the farms, telling everyone. I was sure you would come right back."

"It wasn't easy, but we made it," said Joel, backing out of Mamma's embrace. "I'll tell you more later, over breakfast. I'm starving!" He then turned to shake hands with Herr Ullman.

"Thanks for the adventure. I'll never forget it!"

The schoolmaster shrugged. His tired eyes were ringed with dark smudges and his cheeks looked more hollow than ever. "I'm sorry it didn't work out." He glanced over at Jakob, sleeping in the back seat. "We'd best get home now. We're all exhausted."

"Thank you, thank you," sighed Mamma.

Joel collected his bag and stumbled into the house. He sank into the first chair he saw as Kari hustled into the kitchen for some coffee and rolls. He seriously doubted he had the strength to climb the stairs to bed. One by one, Grandma, Grandpa, and Axel stumbled out to welcome him back.

Three days later, the schoolmaster was back. He had regained the bounce in his step, but his face had a worried cast.

"Fetch your mother, Joel. I have urgent news for the both of you."

A moment later, Mamma emerged on the front step, wiping her hands on a towel.

"Good afternoon, Herr Ullman. Joel tells me you have news. Is something wrong?"

"When were you and Joel planning on going back to America?" he asked abruptly.

Mamma glanced at Joel. "In about ten days. Why do you ask?"

The schoolmaster sighed. "You may be here longer than you had planned, Fru Peterson. I just heard that all the ships are being held in port. Their regular service has stopped. Ships are being used to transport troops now. Even fishing boats have been called in."

Mamma looked stunned. "But we have tickets, bought and paid for!"

Mr. Ullman shook his head. "Believe me, you are not the only ones in this situation. Thousands of travelers all across Europe have tickets they can't use."

"I can't believe it!" said Mamma looking anxiously over at Joel. "We will check with the steamship company in Gothenburg. I am sure something can be arranged."

Herr Ullman climbed back into his buggy. "For both your sakes, I hope so. You must return as soon as you can to America. This ugly war is spreading. Sweden may be neutral now, but the army has started to mobilize. Every able man from twenty-one to forty-two is expected to be ready. That includes me, I'm afraid."

That evening, the church bells began to chime. They continued their slow ringing for three straight hours, spreading a blanket of gloom over the whole countryside.

20
A Small Accident

August 7, 1914

All anyone talks about is the war. The countries of Europe are like children picking sides for a game. England, France, Russia, and Serbia on one side. Germany and Austria-Hungary on the other. The local papers come out with extra editions every day. People can't get enough news. Young men in Germany and England rush to enlist. Bands play as girls throw bouquets to the soldiers leaving by train. Do they think they are going to a party instead of a war? Here in Sweden, we noticed changes right away. People try to go on with their lives anyway. But banks have closed, factories are shut down, and ships don't sail. No mail goes out and none gets in. There are rumors of German subs all along the Norwegian coast. King Gustaf declared Sweden to be neutral, but the people are worried.

After breakfast, Mamma marched downstairs dressed in her dark traveling suit and carrying a carpet bag.

"Going somewhere?" Joel asked.

"Grandpa and I are leaving for Gothenburg," she said.

"What's in Gothenburg?"

"The American consul, for one. You and I are American citizens and we can not be forced to stay in Europe if there's going to be a war."

Joel smiled. She had that 'Boy are you going to get it!' sound to her voice. Like when he got in trouble at home.

"I thought you wanted to stay in Sweden."

"Part of me does want to stay here. I am not at all ready to go back. But we must before things get out of hand." She tugged on her black gloves. "You know the old saying, Joel, *Borta bra, men hemma bäst.*"

"Away is good, but home is best?"

"Exactly. Safe at home in Omaha with Pappa and Linnea." She marched to the door. "Now go get Axel. You two can drive us to the depot and then bring the buggy home."

As much as he wanted to stay and get more information on the war, Joel remembered Pappa was counting on him to get Mamma home. He could still write a story for the paper about their adventures.

Before they left, Kari came out with a small coin purse and handed Joel a shopping list.

"Your grandma says to get what you can. And if there's any money left over, you can buy a little candy."

100

After dropping Grandpa and Mamma at the depot, Axel and Joel stopped at a market in Vetlanda. Prices had jumped on everything in the last few days. They could only get a few of the things Grandma had on her list. The sack of flour took most of the money, up to 60 crowns from 25 before the war. But Joel did have a few *öre* left for some salt licorice.

As the buggy moved slowly down the road home with Pelle plodding lazily along, tiny white butterflies floated around them in the sultry air. From behind them, a loud "Ah-oo-gaaa!" shattered the quiet. Dust and gravel spewed out from a passing automobile. Pelle reared up, then jerked forward, sending the buggy lickety-split down the road.

"Hang on!" yelled Joel, gripping the reins.

They hurtled ahead, bumping and bouncing right past the rude driver. The tin lizzie veered off the road and into a ditch with the driver crying, "Ahhhgahh!"

"Serves him right!" Joel snapped. "Whoa, Pelle, whoa!"

Slowly, they clattered to a stop, dust billowing all around.

"Maybe he's hurt. Let's go see," said Axel, running back to the accident.

When Joel got down, he saw their precious sack of flour splattered in the dirt fifty yards back. Drat! Grandma would not be happy.

"It's Herr Andersson!" yelled Axel.

"Not again!" Joel groaned. Like a stubborn weed, Gunnar kept popping up. He wasn't hurt, but the wheels of his Model-T were stuck deep in the mud.

"Sorry, boys," he muttered. "Just wanted to toot hello to you." He brushed the dirt from his dark suit pants and studied his predicament. He wasn't going anywhere without help.

"I was on my way to look at some property. In fact, it's not far from your farm."

Joel eyed him with suspicion. "Where?"

"I was told to look for an old ruin on a hill. Some place that burned down years ago. I might buy it and build a nice manor house there."

Joel and Axel exchanged knowing looks. Trollbacken! Gunnar Andersson wanted to buy that haunted pile of rocks.

"That's where we went fishing the other day," Joel said. "You'd like it there. View of the lake, lots of..." He searched for the right word.

"Lots of tro—" Axel started to say.

Joel gave him a nudge. "...atmosphere. Don't pay any mind to the rumors about that place, Herr Andersson."

"You mean that legend your mother spoke of?"

"Yeah, you remember, don't you Axel?" Joel wiggled his eyebrows like Grandpa did. "Something about minerals...."

Axel grinned. "Oh, you mean the 'gold and silver and copper' minerals?"

Gunnar's eyes widened. "Gold? I haven't heard any mention of that. You say there's a gold deposit there? And silver, too?"

Joel shrugged. "It's just a fairy tale. Something about trolls guarding their treasure under that rocky hill. You know how it is. Someone probably found something glittery there and made up the story."

Gunnar studied Joel closely. His left eye twitched as he rubbed his chin. "Stories often come from real events. What else do you know about that place, young man?"

"Nothing, sir, not a thing."

Gunnar wagged his finger at Joel. "You just keep it that way. Don't go spreading foolish tales of gold."

Joel stared at the ground so he couldn't see the smile tugging at his cheeks. So, old Mr. Wart-nose hoped there was gold at Trollbacken. Fine! Let him think that. "Come on, Axel. Let's unhitch Pelle and get Herr Andersson out of here. He's got business to take care of!"

It took a few tries, but finally, the sturdy horse hauled the car out of the mud. The right fender was bent a little, but nothing else looked serious.

Gunnar gave the crank a good turn and the car sputtered to life. As he climbed up behind the wheel he added, "Looks like you'll be staying here after all."

"Huh?"

"The war, my dear boy, the war. Hardly any ships going out now. Visitors like you are stuck!"

Joel waved him off. "Oh no. Mamma's taken care of that already. We'll be back home soon."

Gunnar huffed, giving him another doubtful look.

Joel stared back at him, defiant. Well it *could* be true. Mamma might have good news when she got back tomorrow.

"One of the few ships still scheduled to sail is the *Hellig Olav*. I leave on her for America in two weeks. Business, you know."

"Is that so?" Joel tried to sound bored with this news. Gunnar's "business" was probably more shipboard gambling.

Gunnar shifted the Model-T into gear. "I do have an extra ticket. It's worth quite a bit now. I bet your mother would pay anything to send you home, away from all this trouble."

So that's it. Send me back, leave Mamma here, thought Joel. He could feel his anger build. But a voice inside warned him to stay calm, not rise to the bait.

"No, thanks. We'll go together or not at all." He gave a hearty wave goodbye. "Good luck with that property. Maybe you'll strike it rich!"

As the Model-T disappeared down the road, Axel and Joel climbed back on the buggy. The anger Joel had felt a second before had turned to giggles.

"Why are you laughing?" asked Axel.

"I know why he acts like such a troll."

"Why?"

"He's greedy. Did you see his eyes light up at the hint of gold at Trollbacken?"

"We never said there was gold there," Axel protested.

Joel grinned. "Nope, we sure didn't! I forget, did we warn him about the trolls?"

"What trolls?"

Joel gave the reins a snap and Pelle trotted faster. "Trollbacken trolls, of course!"

A short while later, Joel eased the buggy over to the side of the road. Up ahead he could see the black Model-T sitting empty. Like soldiers sneaking up on

the enemy, he and Axel headed for Trollbacken.
They took a short-cut across the rocky field, keeping
low so they wouldn't be seen. As they came over the
rise, Joel could see Gunnar pacing off a section of
land. Nearby, a small camera rested on a granite
rock. Joel pointed to the camera and motioned to
Axel to go get it. Axel scurried over, snatched up the
camera, and was back behind the hill before Gunnar
turned.

"Excellent!" Gunnar said, taking out a pen and
jotting some notes on a small pad. "Lovely view,
plenty of room…" He put the pad and pen down on a
log and went over to inspect a pile of rocks.

Joel edged closer until he was behind a stand of
birch trees. Gunnar stood about five feet away, his
back to them, still examining the rocks. Joel gave
Axel the thumbs up sign and sprinted over to the
log. In a flash, he trotted back to the trees and
waved the pen at Axel.

Gunner turned back to retrieve his pen and pad
but found only the pad. He bent down, searching the
ground. "Ach!" he spluttered. He stood up and
headed for the tree right where Joel was hiding. Joel
felt his heart leap to his throat. Suddenly, Gunnar
stopped, turned, and stared back at the rock where
he'd left the camera.

"What the devil is going on here?" He marched
over and pawed through the tall grass growing by
the rock. As he bent over, a tape measure fell from
his coat pocket. He didn't seem to notice but turned
and retraced his steps back to the log.

Axel darted out, quick as a rabbit, and grabbed
the tape measure. Joel cocked his head letting him

know they'd better skedaddle before they were caught. They bounded across the field, past the ruin of the old forge, and tumbled into the dirt road laughing and coughing. Joel placed the stolen items on the hood of the car where Gunnar couldn't miss them.

21
Going Nowhere

August 8, 1914

I wish I'd gone with Mamma to Gothenburg. It is Sweden's second biggest city. Think of all the war news I could have learned! I hope all went okay. The weather is lousy for traveling. It has rained all night and all day. Axel and I worked on his Erector set a bit. But mostly I've been studying the papers. I don't always understand the words. Today I learned "slagsfelt." It means battlefield. The news reports make it sound like all of Europe will become a "slagsfelt."

"They're here!" Axel shouted.

He dashed out the door to take care of Pelle and the buggy. Mamma and Grandpa sloshed into the house like a couple of drowned chickens. They pulled off their soggy coats and hung them to dry by the cast iron stove.

107

"How did it go?" asked Kari, adding a piece of wood to the fire.

"Not good," said Grandpa.

"Terrible," added Mamma, sinking into a chair. Her hair, usually so neat and tidy, hung in wet clumps around her tired face.

Kari reached for a coffee pot and two mugs. "Here, you need something warm inside you."

"What happened?" asked Joel.

Mamma sighed, taking a cup of coffee from Kari. "It was so crowded. Hundreds of stranded tourists packed the consul's office, all trying to meet with Mr. Sawyer."

"What did he say?"

"He was very nice, very kind to everyone," said Mamma.

"A gibbering old hen, he was!" Grandpa waved his arms in disgust.

"He was trying his best," said Mamma. "Mr. Sawyer told everyone to take any passage they could find and get home quickly. The problem is, there are only six steamers leaving now from Copenhagen and Christiania. And they are all fully booked."

"Nothing until November," added Grandpa.

Joel was confused. "November? What about our tickets?"

Mamma shook her head slowly. "Our tickets home were on the *Vaterland*, a German ship. It's being held in New Jersey by our government."

The facts of their situation smacked him like a wet rag. Pappa had booked them on the *Vaterland* because they had planned to see some of Denmark and Germany before coming home. He didn't want to believe it, but Gunnar and Mr. Ullman had been right. They were stuck.

Grandpa pulled out a hanky and handed it to Mamma who had started to cry silently. Then he added, "We met a man who offered a thousand dollars to someone in Copenhagen for their third-class ticket. He didn't get it. Imagine! A thousand dollars!"

"That's another problem for us," said Mamma. "No one will cash our traveler's checks. We have no money for new tickets if they landed in our laps." She buried her face in her hands. "Heaven help us! I could float all the way home on these tears!"

Joel gulped. So much for buying Gunnar's ticket. He probably wanted two thousand for it. It might as well be a million.

"I have never felt so helpless," sobbed Mamma. She looked up at Joel, her eyes hopeful.

But he didn't have any answers. Frustration gnawed at him like a rat on an old shoe. Pappa had given him a job to do. Get Mamma to Sweden and home again. But no one had guessed a war would break out. How would he prove he could make good decisions now? Plans for their trip had been yanked out of his hands. He'd tried to send a cable home a few days ago. Sorry, no personal wires allowed.

But Pappa must know we are stuck, thought Joel. He's sitting at home reading the Omaha paper and saying, 'Joel will figure something out.' And I will! Somehow. He looked anxiously over at Kari, wondering what would happen to her. She was sure safer here than in Christiania, especially away from Uncle Ivar.

Axel came in the kitchen and scooted next to Joel on the bench. "Did you tell them about Herr Andersson?"

"You saw Gunnar?" asked Mamma, looking up.

"We sort of had an accident on the road. He landed in the ditch," said Axel with a grin.

"Whaaat?" Mamma cried.

"It was all his fault," Joel quickly added. "He was tearing down the road in that automobile of his. He's okay. Nothing broken." He glared at Axel, hoping he'd keep his big mouth shut about Gunnar's run-in with two "trolls."

That night, Joel lay awake trying to figure out how to get home. He feared the longer they waited, the harder it would be to get back. A chill went up his spine remembering something he'd read in the paper. Every day the Germans laid more mines in the North Sea. Torpedo boats patrolled all along the Norwegian coast. What if they did get on a ship, and what if that ship hit a mine? Would staying in Sweden be better than risking the sea? And for how long?

Homesickness opened its big ugly mouth and swallowed him whole. In Swedish they called it "home longing." Now, with his eyes squeezed shut, he longed for Omaha—the stink of the stockyards, the fireflies dancing in the humid night air, and the clanging of streetcars. He could almost hear the tinkle of piano notes as Linnea gave lessons in the parlor. He stared blindly into the darkness of the attic room, thoughts pounding in his head. How do you solve a problem as big as this? His father's challenge echoed in his head: *Prove you are old enough to make big decisions!* Yes, but how?

Sitting up, he punched his pillow. It wasn't fair! thought Joel. How come Gunnar Andersson had tickets to America? He must have won them gambling. There must be a way to get those tickets. Both of them. One ticket wouldn't do. And if he couldn't buy them, was there some other way to get them? An idea wormed its way into his brain as a smile crept across his face. Slowly, a glimmer of hope glowed in the night, chasing away the dark.

Marianne Olson

22
Setting Traps

August 10, 1914

The chance to try out his plan came two days
later. It was _kräftor_ season in Sweden, and time for
another feast. Everywhere the small lakes teemed
with tiny crayfish. Traps had to be set in the water
at dusk and collected in the morning. Back home in
Omaha, Joel had caught crayfish in the pond by the
power plant. If he got a good haul, he sold them for a
quarter a bucket.

That night, just as it was getting dark, Grandpa,
Joel, and Axel hiked to the lake at Trollbacken to set
the traps. The full moon cast an eerie glow over the
landscape, turning tree stumps and rocks into
fearsome shadows. As they got closer, Joel saw some
large thing moving around in the ruins. The hair on
the back of his neck bristled. He watched as the
thing staggered around slowly. Then it stopped,

mumbled something, and moved on. Joel glanced over at Axel, whose eyes bulged out in fright.

"Wheeet!" Grandpa whistled.

The figure jumped, then lunged toward them, a glowing red coal in its head.

"You scared the wits out of me!" it said, coming closer.

Cigar smoke floated in the air. Gunnar again!

"We thought you were a troll!" panted Axel.

"You don't believe all that malarkey, do you?" Gunnar asked, bending down and pawing tufts of grass.

"Did you lose something?" Joel asked.

"Yes, confound it! The other day I lost—or thought I had lost—several personal items." He glanced sharply at Axel who blinked, confused.

"Most of the things turned up, like magic, on the hood of my car."

Most things? wondered Joel. He knew he had returned everything—pen, camera, and tape measure. A common thief he was not.

"Lost my silver pen," Gunner added, staring now directly at Joel.

"We don't have it, honest!" blurted out Axel.

"What are you doing out here in the dark?" interrupted Grandpa.

Gunnar stood up, his manner turning business-like. "I'd like to buy this fine piece of property. Maybe build a nice house overlooking the lake. I understand you're the owner, Herr Johansson."

"*Ja,* but it's not for sale," huffed Grandpa, dismissing him and heading toward the lake. Axel followed him, trotting like a puppy dog.

"But, but...."

"Not for sale!" repeated Grandpa .

Gunnar tossed his still glowing cigar on the ground. "Stubborn old man! He wants it himself!"

Joel's guess had been right. Gunnar really had his heart set on getting this land. He must believe there's gold on it. Greed was his weakness all right. All day Joel had been working on a plan, a way to trip up Gunnar and get the tickets. But there hadn't been time to talk his plan over with Grandpa. He had to gamble now it would work.

"We're setting traps for the crayfish tonight," Joel explained, "for a big dinner tomorrow."

Gunnar grunted, not caring to discuss crayfish or anything else. He kept staring after Grandpa.

"Perhaps you'd like to join us? About four o'clock?" Joel held his breath, hoping he would say 'yes.' "If you really want this property, I think I can talk Grandpa into selling."

Gunnar turned around slowly, his eyes boring into Joel. "You think so, do you?" He fidgeted again with the coins in his pocket. "I'll be over at four." And without another word, he marched off into the night.

Joel went over to stomp on the cigar ash before it started a fire. Something long and silver glinted in the grass nearby. When he looked closer, he saw it was Gunnar's pen.

Now how did that get there? He decided to leave the pen right where it was. As he headed down toward the lake to join Grandpa and Axel, he peered into the shadows, wondering if trolls were really hiding in them.

114

23
All That Glitters

August 11, 1914

"No! Never in this life will I sell to that man!"

"But Grandpa, why not? It may be the only way Mamma and I can get home!" Joel had picked the privacy of the woodshed to plead his case. He had to convince Grandpa to go along with the plan. If he didn't, Joel knew they'd be stuck.

"Two reasons. First, I don't want that no-account cheat for a neighbor." Grandpa tapped his pipe on the edge of the stump, emptying out the old tobacco. "Second, if he builds a house there, I won't be able to fish in the lake. And I dearly love that lake!" Grandpa chomped hard on the end of his pipe, his expression set like stone.

This was turning out to be harder than Joel had expected. He took a deep breath and tried to reason with Grandpa again. "I don't think he'll be building a house there. He's got some crazy idea there's gold at Trollbacken."

"Where'd he hear that?"

Joel coughed. "Well...uh...Axel and I, we...we started to tell him the story you told us. Axel blurted out the gold and silver and copper part."

Grandpa made a face. "Joel, you didn't tell lies, did you?"

"He only wants the land so he can dig it up."

Grandpa snorted. "Dig it up? Ha! That hill is nothing but rocks. He'll be digging for twenty years! And making a mess to boot!"

"I doubt he'll stick around that long. He's a get-rich-quick kind of guy, remember?"

Grandpa stuffed new tobacco in his pipe, knitting his bushy eyebrows together as he worked. After a long pause he leaned forward, poking Joel's chest with the bowl of his pipe. "How do you know those tickets are any good? I'm not giving up that land for some flim-flam deal!"

"I'll check them out before you sign anything. No tickets, no deal." Even as he said it, Joel wasn't sure exactly how he could check them out. He'd figure that part out later.

Grandpa sat back, picked up a block of wood and whittled a bit. "It's true you and Annali are in a fix. And it's true I'd do anything to help you get home. But I don't like this idea. Not one bit." Silence filled the tiny woodshed like the smoke from Grandpa's pipe. The old man kept his eyes on the chunk of wood, chipping away a piece here and another there.

Joel thought it best to let him be. He got up, went outside and strolled over to the edge of the yard. What he would do if Grandpa wouldn't sell? How would he get those tickets? He let his eyes wander across the lower field. Down below, the old church tower pointed to the sky. Joel tried to imagine his mother sitting in that church before she left for America. She was a young girl then, about his age, facing a dangerous trip across the sea all by herself. What prayers were said? What prayers should he say now? What would happen if they couldn't get home? What would Pappa say if he failed? How long he stared across the field, he didn't know. A pungent feather of pipe smoke interrupted his thoughts.

Grandpa stood next to him and placed his pipe on the stone wall. "You know I'd much rather keep you and Annali here a bit longer. But this war may spread. Maybe it is best to get you two on a ship now."

Joel let out the breath he'd been holding and wrapped his arms around the old man. "Thanks, Grandpa. Now cross your fingers he'll go for our asking price."

Grandpa laughed and held up his gnarly fists, thumbs tucked inside. "Here in Sweden we say 'hold your thumbs' for good luck."

Joel had invited Gunnar to come at four, not six, the usual dinner time, because he knew Mamma, Kari, and Grandma would be visiting at the neighbor's house for coffee. Win or lose, he had to make this deal on his own. If he lost, Mamma would never have to know about it. He wouldn't want her to know how close they had come.

Right on time, Gunnar's black Model-T sputtered into the yard. He hopped out and strode straight to the front door. As usual, he had spiffed himself up and reeked of cologne.

"Come on in, Herr Andersson," Joel said, leading him into the parlor.

Grandpa rocked silently in his old chair, looking sour, his hands clenched across his stomach. Joel prayed he wouldn't go back on his agreement.

"Mamma's not here right now," he explained. "We can take care of our business first thing."

Gunnar nodded, taking off his straw hat, turning it nervously in his hands as he spoke. "Fine with me!" Then to Grandpa he said, "Good day, Herr Johansson. I hope you have reconsidered about that piece of land."

Grandpa merely rocked, saying nothing, letting Gunnar wait.

"I'm prepared to offer you a tidy sum for it. Such a shame to let it sit there, unused."

More silence from Grandpa.

"So....ah...," Gunnar turned to Joel, his brow wrinkled. "You did talk to him, didn't you? Will he sell?"

Joel stuck his hands deep in his pockets like he'd seen Pappa do when he talked serious business. "Well, that depends. We have a certain price in mind."

"Name it!"

He paused, pretending he was still thinking it over. "Do you still have those steamship tickets you mentioned the other day? Both of them?"

"Yes...I do." Gunnar reached into his jacket and drew out a long, thick envelope. "Got them right here, in fact."

"May I see them?" Joel asked, reaching for the envelope. He pulled out the papers and studied them. They looked a lot like the tickets he and Mamma used when they came over. Same Danish company, the Scandinavian American Line. Ship's name: *Hellig Olav*. Date of departure: 21 August 1914 from Christiania to New York. One detail was different. These were first-class tickets! Joel's heart beat so hard, he was sure Gunnar could hear it. Keep cool, keep cool, he kept telling himself. If these tickets are good, Mamma and I will be home soon.

"Here's the deal, Herr Andersson," he said, taking his time and trying not to sound too eager. "My grandfather will sell the land at Trollbacken in exchange for both these tickets...provided they check out with the steamship company."

"And one thousand Swedish crowns!" added Grandpa.

"Oh, the tickets are good, no doubt about it," insisted Gunnar. "How soon can you decide?"

"Leave the tickets here today," Joel said. "If everything is in order, we'll have the papers ready tomorrow."

"Must you have both the tickets?"

"Absolutely. It's a small price to pay for that beautiful lake property, don't you agree?"

Gunnar beamed like a cat with a platter of fish. "Yes, of course! Both tickets, plus one thousand crowns." He hurried over and pumped Grandpa's hand, saying, "This is wonderful! Just wonderful!"

Grandpa couldn't look him in the eye. Joel knew how hard it was for him to give up his favorite fishing spot. Finally, Grandpa muttered, *"Ja, ja,* if you think so."

Gunnar reached for Joel's hand and this time gave him a proper handshake, one that didn't hurt. "I must hurry out to see the property again. Please give my excuses to your mother, Joel. I won't be staying for dinner after all."

As soon as he left, Joel ran all the way down to the post office in Stentorp where he knew there was a telephone. The postmaster helped him place a call to the steamship company in Gothenburg. After describing the tickets in detail, he got the information he needed. They were as good as gold!

24
Sad Farewells

Aug. 12-21, 1914

We didn't tell anyone about the tickets until the deal was done. Gunnar met us in Vetlanda as we had planned and handed over the thousand Swedish crowns. Grandpa signed the papers giving Gunnar the land. The two men hardly spoke to each other. Then Gunnar hurried away without even wishing Mamma and me a safe trip. Some old friend! When I showed Mamma the tickets, she nearly cried. She said, "My little goose has plucked the old rooster!" Now we really have to hurry. We must be in Christiania by the 21st.

The days flew by as Joel and Mamma rushed to get packed. Grandma found little things around the house for them to take back home. Two small copper pots, some weavings, and several pressed flowers to remind Mamma of Solgården.

Kari and Joel managed a few moments alone out in the apple orchard. She pulled a paper from her apron and unfolded it.

"It's a drawing of us on the boat," she said.

"It's great! I'll hang it in my room."

"I love the music box you brought me. I play the little tune each night before I go to bed."

Joel squeezed her hand. "You said once I was sneaky. Well, that's my sneaky way of making sure you don't forget me."

Kari tried a brief smile, but her lips soon began trembling and her eyes filled with tears.

"Don't cry, Kari."

"But I'm scared!"

"You'll be all right here with—"

"Not for me, silly. I'm scared for you!"

"For me?"

"For you and your mother and all those other people on the ship. What if you hit a mine? What if a torpedo—?" She fought back the tears as she leaned her head against his shoulder.

Joel put his arm around her and buried his face in her splendid red hair. What could he say to make her feel better? He felt pretty rotten, too, leaving her behind. His heart ached knowing how she'd rather be going with them back to America. Silently, he made a promise to get her back to America someday.

"Here you are!" Axel came bounding out, breaking the spell. "I have a going-away gift for you," he announced. He whipped off his blue wool cap and plopped it on Joel's head. "For that, you send me some comics so I can learn English. Then I'll come visit you!"

Two days later, it was time to go. Uncle Johan came over from Falkenberg to collect Axel and to drive Joel and his mother to the train station. He brought along a small camera. Everyone lined up by one of the apple trees for a photo. Afterward, Mamma clung to Grandma and Grandpa for several minutes, not wanting to say a final goodbye. "One more time in life," Grandma had said. And that's what she got.

Joel couldn't decide how he felt. He was sad to be leaving, happy to be going home. And certain he'd be back soon. He had it all planned out. The war would end soon. The governments would settle their problems and bring the soldiers home. In four years he'd be done with high school. Then he'd come back for Kari.

As the buggy pulled out of Solgården, Joel turned and looked back, memorizing the scene—Grandma and Grandpa by their little red house, Kari waving her apron in circles over her head.

The buggy had almost reached the end of the stone fence when he had an idea. "Stop, Johan! I forgot something!" He jumped down and ran to the fence. A stone, the size of a baseball, seemed just right. He pried it loose and jumped back onto his seat.

"What on earth?" Mamma stared down at his prize.

"A souvenir. Now we'll always have a piece of Sweden with us!"

"Oh, no," said Johan. "We'll miss that stone. You'll have to return and bring it back!"

Joel stuck out his hand. "It's a deal!"

The train from Vetlanda took them back over the mountains to Norway. Christiania hummed like a different city since the war broke out. Now, anxious travelers, mostly Americans, jammed the harbor trying to get on a ship. Refugees, clutching their few belongings, stood in long lines with millionaires, all hoping for tickets.

Joel and his mother spent the entire morning at the ship, getting their bags inspected and making sure their names were on the passenger list. A doctor checked them for any disease. The last thing needed on a crowded ship was someone with small pox or tuberculosis.

Mamma had hoped to board right away, but Joel had an errand to do first.

"Kari asked me to stop in at Café Bryggan and tell her uncle how she was doing," he explained. "It will only take a few minutes."

Mamma squeezed her eyes shut, her face taut with worry. "Please hurry, then! The ship is overbooked and I do not want to lose our places!"

Joel wormed his way through the crowd and ran across the street to the café. Uncle Ivar was surprised to see him, but glad to hear Kari was doing fine.

When he came back outside, Joel noticed the air had a chill to it. The sky had turned an ashy shade of gray as if dusk had fallen in the middle of the day.

"What's going on?"

Uncle Ivar looked up, squinting at the sky. A dark splotch covered most of the sun. "It's a solar eclipse," he said. "Not a good omen. You'd best get back to the ship. People get nervous when this happens."

Joel's heart pounded as he hurried back to the pier. Uncle Ivar had been right. The eclipse had sent a wave of panic through the throng of people. Like lemmings to the sea, they pushed and shoved toward the boat. Babies cried, mothers called out to older children, gathering them in close.

But where was Mamma? His heart skipped a beat as he scanned the sea of faces, searching for her. He tried to inch forward, but bundles and suitcases blocked the way. He knew how worried Mamma must be with him gone. Finding a break between bodies, he shoved on through. Elbows poked him. He tripped over someone's boots, but he kept on moving. He wasn't even sure he was heading in the right direction. Just keep on moving, he told himself, just keep moving. Whatever you do, Joel, don't get lost!

25

Dangerous Waters

August 21-24, 1914

Joel gasped for breath, his nose and mouth pressed against a stout passenger's rough coat. He dropped down to leg level, took a deep breath and sprang out like a rabbit from a hole. The sudden movement startled the people around him, allowing him to escape. Finally, he spotted Mamma's dark feathered hat sticking up above the crowd.

"I'm coming!" he shouted, pushing his way toward her.

"Thank God!" cried Mamma.

He grabbed her gloved hand. "Come on. Let's go home now."

Bad omens or not, everyone cheered when the steamer left port and headed down the fjord to the sea. This time, Joel and his mother had a bigger, fancier cabin with a nice sofa. But because the ship was oversold, they had to share it with an elderly woman from Belgium who spoke only French. Some passengers had to sleep in the baggage hold. To make room for them, a mountain of trunks and bundles had been left behind on the pier. Joel hoped theirs wasn't among them.

As soon as the steamer entered the North Sea, the weather turned nasty. Ragged clouds shoved across the gray sky as winds tore the rain out of them. It seemed they made little or no progress. The steamer crept along, with crewmen posted on all sides, scanning the water for mines. Captain Holst came on the speakers and announced a warning, first in Danish, then in English. He told the passengers they were in for a rough ride. He explained that they were turning north, up the Norwegian coast, where they could be clear of mines in the sea lanes. It would take longer this way, but it would also be safer.

Seasickness clobbered Joel and Mamma right away. Joel left the ladies the privacy of the cabin and trudged down the hall to the forward lounge. Through the windows he could see angry green waves lashing at the decks, smashing chairs and sweeping them out to sea. The sight of rolling mountains of water capped with foam made his whole body quiver. He braced against the wall, keeping his eyes focused straight ahead. The bow plunged abruptly into the sea, sending water cascading all over and making the steamer stand on end. The jolt sent him sprawling to the floor. It wasn't enough to get tickets home, thought Joel. We still have to survive the trip across the Atlantic, too!

By the second day, they had made the port of Christiansand where they sat out the worst of the storm. From there, they headed west, clear of the mined areas. But not yet clear of danger.

To Joel's surprise, his old friend Jon, from the wireless room, was now working on this ship. He found him by the rail, scanning the horizon with binoculars.

"Hey, remember me?" Joel asked, tapping him on the arm. "I came over with you in June."

Jon turned, his ruddy face breaking into a broad smile. "Sure. We sent a cablegram for your girl-friend."

"Yeah, Kari." He gulped, missing her already. "So... what were you looking at?"

"See those seagulls out there?" He pointed off the starboard side.

Joel could see about fifty or sixty seagulls swooping over a certain spot in the water. "What's out there, food?" he asked.

"Food from a submarine, most likely," said Jon. "They can see the sub under the water. It's a dead giveaway."

"Think it's a German sub? A U-boat?"

"Don't know. Could be German. Could also be British. We'll have to wait and see."

They didn't have to wait for long. Thirty minutes later, the sub surfaced, looking like a long steel coffin. There was movement on the topside. Then popping firecracker sounds of a machine gun. Joel hit the deck, his heart in his throat. What were they doing?

The shooting missed them, but the response was immediate. The *Hellig Olav's* engines groaned as the ship slowed to a stop. The U-boat signaled. Jon signaled back. Jon explained that they were asking what country this ship was from and where it was headed. They also asked to board for inspection.

"Why doesn't the captain tell them to go to the devil?" asked Joel.

Jon laughed. "In normal times he could. But these are not normal times. On our way over from America, we were stopped and searched by the British."

"What were they looking for?"

"Contraband, war materials, anything that might help the other side," explained Jon. "It does not matter what flag you are flying or what direction you are headed."

"They sound like pirates, to me!"

Jon shook his head. "No, they will follow the rules. If they don't find anything, they will let us go. If they decide we are a threat, we will be given a chance to abandon the ship before they sink it."

"Sink it!" Joel felt his mouth go dry and his stomach twist. "Good grief! Why did we pick this summer to travel?"

"Don't worry," said Jon, putting his arm on his shoulder. "It'll be all right."

But he did worry. He imagined what it would be like, getting blown to bits by a torpedo. Would they die at once, or would they drift for days in a life boat in the middle of the ocean? He wished he didn't have such a vivid imagination.

When the noisy engines of the steamer went silent, curious passengers gathered on deck to see what was happening.

A small dinghy nosed up to the side of the ship. Two German officers, dressed from head to toe in black, climbed up the ladder, guns at their sides. One man wore an eye patch, making him look even more sinister. They talked with the captain and the first officer. It all seemed so polite, but everyone knew it wasn't a friendly visit. The Germans checked some papers and then started to inspect the ship, including the cargo. Joel wondered if they would paw through their trunks, all stuffed with dirty underwear.

There was nothing to do but wait. To pass the time, Jon related a story about a recent sinking. A German sub had stopped a cargo ship headed for England. They allowed the crew to get into life boats before sending a torpedo into the cargo ship and sinking it. Then the Germans towed the life boats closer to shore so that all would be rescued. All very civilized. Joel wondered if it was true.

After a couple of hours, the Germans were done. They found no guns, no piles of scarce fuel. But as Eye-Patch started to leave, Joel caught a glimpse of a familiar brown leather journal tucked under his arm.

"Hey!" Joel called out, lunging forward.

Jon grabbed his arm, jerking him back. "Stay put, you fool!"

Eye-Patch turned and pointed his Luger at Joel. "You are having a problem?"

Joel flinched at the sight of the gun. "You—you have my journal."

Eye Patch glanced at the leather book. "So, you are the one sending this war information back to America?"

Joel shook his head. "No, no. It's only notes about our visit to Grandma and...."

"You don't write this about tourist visits!" Eye Patch jabbed his finger at the skull and cross-bones Joel had sketched on the first page along with the words: "Keep out!" and "Top Secret."

Silly. A silly, childish drawing. It didn't mean a thing. Joel clamped his mouth shut. Maybe if the Germans thought they had some important spy material there, they'd be satisfied and go their way.

Eye Patch slowly tucked the gun back in his jacket. He turned to the captain. "Be careful! We might come back!" Then he and his partner eased down the ladder to their waiting dinghy.

Joel's fists stayed clenched until the sub slipped away, belching out ugly diesel smoke as it went. Even though there seemed to be rules about sinking passenger ships, four of the crew stationed themselves fore and aft, watching out for torpedo trails.

For the next two days, Joel joined the men, scanning the water for signs of trouble. Off and on, he and Jon spotted the outline of a ship on the horizon. They couldn't tell what kind it was, only that it was following them.

Sometimes he would go as far forward as he could on the ship and let the wind and sea spray prickle his skin. His nerves jumped like grasshoppers in a field but the salty air eased his fears. Other times he wanted to dive in the ocean and push the ship as fast as he could to New York.

The ship steamed ahead, putting hundreds of miles between the passengers and the war zone. But unlike the trip in June, there were no festive parties at night. This time they crossed the Atlantic in darkness with the lights out and the portholes covered. Even this far away, subs could be lurking. On a visit to the wireless room Joel learned it, too, was silent. There'd be no messages sent to give away their position. It was as if they were sneaking home, running from the neighborhood bully.

During the day, the ship's orchestra gave concerts on the deck. Mamma said it was to take away the worry about the Germans. During one concert, Joel found her snuggled in blankets on a chair. She took his hand and gave it a pat.

"I am sorry those awful men took your notes, Joel," she said.

"I still have some scribbled notes. And Jon gave me more paper." He held out a pad of paper for her to see. The top of each sheet had the name of the ship and the insignia of the Scandinavian American Line. "I'm starting a new journal and re-writing what was lost."

"Good for you!"

"And, I've been interviewing the passengers about their experiences. I already have some great stories." He flipped open his notes to show her. "One lady couldn't stop crying. She had to leave everything, including her old basset hound, behind in Paris.

Another man told me he'd escaped from a German prison to get here. And Jon said that soon after we left, two Danish cargo ships struck mines in the North Sea and sank."

"Oh, dear!" Mamma gasped. "Maybe you should not tell me any more news. It is so awful!"

Joel glanced around at the other passengers. "Uncle Karl told me that news is really stories about people. Every person here is a story! "

Mamma smiled. "Then you get busy, my little goose. Off you go!"

The pride in her voice sent a warm glow through Joel. But he still worried about what Pappa's decision would be. Had he proven himself on this trip? Or would all the complications of the war work against him? In the end, would Pappa still insist he come to work in the tailor shop?

26
Icebergs and Fog

August 28, 1914

Day eight. Because of the threat of mines and subs, the ship has followed a northern route, past Iceland and Greenland. Now we are stuck in a dense fog and going nowhere. Just as well. I heard someone say we were near a field of icebergs. Good grief! I can't stop thinking about the Titanic. She's out here somewhere, way, way down. I wonder what she looks like? Are there bones and jewels and trunks full of money trapped in the wreckage?

"Oooooooo-ahhhhhhhh!"

The sudden bellowing of the foghorn gave Joel a start. The ship sounded like a love-sick whale, calling to its mate. The loudspeaker in the lounge crackled to life and Captain Holst announced a lifeboat drill. Joel folded his notes into his coat and hurried to find Mamma. He found her pacing back and forth by life boat station seven, panic in her face.

"What now?" she moaned.

"It's only for practice," he said, trying to sound calm. The captain had stopped the ship. Other passengers joined them, trussed up in life belts, chatting idly. No one talked about the *Hellig Olav* being "unsinkable." After the *Titanic,* no one dared. Joel's gut feelings told him they weren't far from that fatal spot.

Worry filled Mama's eyes. "Maybe the captain doesn't want to tell us what's happening. Maybe the Germans are back."

Joel jerked his head toward the fog. "If they are, they sure can't see us in this!"

The drill turned out to be a regular night-shirt parade. It had caught some people sleeping and they now stumbled out in bathrobes and slippers. A gruff voice caught Joel's attention.

"A damned nuisance, I tell you!" muttered an older man as he struggled with his life belt. "This is the last time I bother to cross the pond to Europe!"

Another man agreed. "I want to plant my two feet on the good old U.S. of A. I only hope Wilson sticks to his promise to keep us out of their stupid war!"

"Yes indeed! Let them settle their own squabbles. It's none of our business."

Joel cringed, hearing them talk like that. He didn't want America in the war, either. But he had family over there. And Kari. It mattered a lot what happened to them. What if Sweden got invaded? What if...what if they got killed? He pushed that thought out of his mind. Think positive. Plan ahead, he told himself.

By noon the next day, the fog had lifted, revealing blue-gray chunks of ice floating about a mile away. Joel remembered what his teacher had said about icebergs. Only a small part stuck out of the water. Much more floated beneath the surface. Pretty to look at, but deadly. Joel and everyone else sighed cautiously when the steamer finally nosed away from them.

Every day after that, he checked their progress on a chart in the wireless room. He made a note in his new journal: average distance traveled was about three-hundred miles a day. But these last miles seemed to take forever.

One afternoon, Jon informed Joel it was now safe to send cablegrams. Joel grabbed a notepad and dashed off two messages. One to Pappa letting him know they were coming and one to Uncle Karl. His job of getting Mamma home was almost done. Would Pappa be proud of him? Would agree he was old enough to make decisions? Would Uncle Karl have a new job waiting?

Finally, on the eleventh day, the lighthouse at Narragansett, Rhode Island, loomed off the port bow. Joel pushed his way through the passengers who had gathered on the second-class deck for a glimpse of home.

"Yahoo!" He ran to tell Mamma the news.

That night, the captain gave a fancy party for all the passengers complete with funny paper hats, horns to toot, and streamers to throw. For the first time, all the lights blazed on the ship. Now that the ship was close to home shores, the air of nervous tension lifted.

In spite of the festive mood, Joel noticed that Mamma was quiet. When she left the dinner table and strolled out to the deck, he followed her.

He found her leaning on the rail, staring up at the starry sky. The Big Dipper hung in its usual place, off to the north. Moonlight flickered across the waves like silver butterflies.

"Are you sad?" he asked.

"A little," she replied, her voice soft. "Travel is so hard. This will probably be the last time I cross the ocean, the last time I see my family. But I am happy we went, in spite of all the trouble. Never take your family for granted, Joel. Even if there are miles between you, they are still part of you."

Joel nodded. "I used to think Grandma and Grandpa were so far away they weren't real. But now they have voices and hugs and funny stories. I liked them!"

She looked away quickly from him, but not before he saw a tear roll down her cheek. He felt in his pocket for Pappa's watch. His goodbye seemed like only yesterday. An old worry came back to haunt him.

"Are you glad to be coming home to Pappa?"

She turned to him, her head bowed. "And why would you think I wasn't?"

He gulped. "Before we left, I know you and Pappa argued a lot...you were so unhappy!"

Mamma folded him into her arms. "No, no, no. Married people have arguments sometimes. I was homesick, Joel. I needed to see my family one more time in life."

"Is that all?"

She paused, a determined look in her eye. "There are other things I want. For one, I would like to get a job. I am a pretty good bookkeeper, you know. And I would like a chance to have my voice heard. Women should not have to keep their opinions a secret. We should have a vote. And we certainly should have a say about important things, like war."

She looked Joel full in the face, her gray eyes fixed on his. "This trip showed me how much I had changed since emigrating, Joel. I am not a meek Swedish farm girl anymore. I am an American. I must take advantage of my freedoms. Your pappa will just have to get used to it!"

She pushed Joel out at arm's length. "You have grown up on this trip. He will have to get used to your independence, too."

He studied her face for a few seconds. She did look a lot more self-assured and confident. "Do you think Pappa will? Do you think he'll let me decide for myself what I want?"

"We'll find out soon, won't we?" she said.

27
Home Again

September 2, 1914

The next morning, under a clear blue sky, the *Hellig Olav* steamed up the Hudson River. When it passed the Statue of Liberty, Joel took off Axel's blue cap and waved to her.

"We're back! Did you miss us?" he yelled.

Once again the pier was a mass of people, ships bellowing and tooting, and horns honking. After clearing customs, Mamma and Joel headed out into the great hall. Their next stop was to be the train depot to get tickets to Omaha. But a small man with a familiar handlebar mustache rushed over to them.

"Welcome back, my little family!" cried Pappa, his face beaming.

"Alfred!" Mamma rushed into his outstretched arms. "We did not expect to see you here!"

"I was so worried. I had to come." He turned and gave Joel a hug, too. "Thank you, son, for sending the cable. How did you manage to get back? The papers have been full of stories of stranded Americans."

Mamma put her arm around Joel's shoulder, saying, "He arranged everything! You would not believe what a clever son we have. A gentleman and a scholar!"

Pappa studied him, his face serious once again. "Is that so? I had a call from your uncle at the paper. You sent him a cable, too? Something about a story?"

Joel took a deep breath, hoping Pappa wasn't going to be angry. "Yes, about the war. What did Uncle say?"

His father's stern manner melted into a broad grin. "They want to talk with you as soon as you get back! So, I thought, why not call the *Omaha Posten?* And they are interested in a story, too."

A rush of excitement filled Joel from head to toe. It was worth the whole trip to see the pride in Pappa's face. Two papers wanting his story! But his enthusiasm cooled as a small worry rose in his head.

"But the *Omaha Posten*... it's all in Swedish. I'm not sure I can write well enough in Swedish."

Pappa put his hands on his shoulders. "I will help you. You will do fine!"

Joel couldn't keep from blurting out the question burning in his mind. "What about working at your shop?"

His father stuck his hands deep in his pockets, scanning Joel from head to toe. "Sometimes plans have to be adjusted. You cannot make a tall man fit into short trousers. You have kept your part of the bargain. I am proud of you, Joel, very proud."

140

Joel beamed. He'd done it!

Pappa turned to Mamma, pressing her hands between his own. "Linnea sends her love. We managed all right while you were away."

"As I knew you would," said Mamma.

"But now, thank God, you are home. Things can get back to normal again."

Mamma linked her arm through his. "Maybe not quite so normal. We will talk about it."

She glanced sideways at Joel and winked.

28
Extra! Extra!

October 4 , 1914

A cold rain drizzled down Joel's neck as he stood under the lamp post in front of the City Market on Jackson Street. The stack of papers at his feet represented his humble beginnings in the newspaper business. By now he'd gotten his first taste of being a published author, too. His articles on the war had appeared in the *World-Herald* under the headline, "Eyewitness in Berlin," and in the Swedish paper as, "Worries in the Homeland." Pappa had been so proud, he showed them off to all who came into his shop. He even framed the articles and hung them in the parlor at home.

Joel had agreed to work a few hours a week at the tailor shop, waiting on customers and taking inventory. He didn't have to be a tailor, but he could still learn how a business worked. And Pappa had asked him to write up advertisements for the newspaper.

He reached in his pocket. There was just enough light to read the letter he'd gotten from Kari yesterday. He'd read it over so many times, he had it memorized. It still made him laugh.

September 1, 1914
Solgården

Dear Joel,

By the time you get this, you will be home. I hope you had a good crossing. We are all fine here. Grandma is teaching me to weave. Grandpa sends greetings, too. Soon after you left, we heard an awful explosion. Gunnar got so impatient digging for his "gold," he decided to use dynamite instead.

When Grandpa got to Trollbacken, he saw Gunnar had blown away the hill, making a huge hole. The explosion hit an underground spring, filling the hole with water until it joined with the lake. Gunnar was so furious, he left town. We heard he was looking for new adventures in the Swedish army!

Grandpa is thrilled. Now he has a bigger lake to fish in and no Gunnar for a neighbor. I worried about the trolls. Did they get blown up, too?

Grandpa said not even dynamite could hurt them. He thinks they are now dancing at the bottom of the lake. Write soon! Greet your mother from me.

Your friend,
Kari

Joel tucked the letter safely back under his rain slicker. Some days, Sweden seemed as far away as

143

the moon to him. He hoped everyone would stay safe over there. He glanced at the headline on the morning paper at his feet. Two Danish ships had just been sunk in the North Sea. The fighting was spreading. Thousands of soldiers were dying. He feared things would get a lot worse before they got better. With Sweden staying out of the war, Kari should be okay, taking care of Grandma and Grandpa. Was she sitting in her attic room, the room where he had stayed, listening to her music box and its plinkity tune?

"I won't let you down, Kari," he whispered to himself. "I'll write every week so you don't forget me. And every day I'll work on plans for the next trip—the trip to bring you home again."

AUTHOR'S NOTE

When war broke out in August of 1914, nearly 100,000 Americans found themselves stranded on foreign soil. They faced many of the same problems as Joel and his mother in getting home again. The problem was so great, Congress passed legislation to provide funds to help get our citizens back. The battle cruiser *Tennessee* was dispatched to bring Americans safely across the channel to England where they hoped to get passage to America.

Travelers during that summer had good reason to worry about sea travel. Several merchant ships were early victims of mines and torpedoes in the North Sea. In the spring of 1915, a German torpedo hit the luxury liner, *Lusitania*, off the coast of Ireland. The ship sank, costing 1,198 lives, including 128 Americans.

At the start of the war, many believed it would be over quickly, by Christmas at the latest. But some European governments decided this was the time to settle old conflicts. The war spread around the world as country after country took up arms. The young soldiers and their recruiters thought it would be a grand and glorious adventure, over and done with in a few months. On both points, they were dreadfully wrong.

World War I erased the old ideas about fighting the enemy in an "honorable" way. New and more horrible forms of warfare made their debut. Some of these new methods included the wide use of armored tanks, poison gas, machine guns, aerial bombings, submarines, and torpedoes. Those who so eagerly marched off to war in 1914 had no idea what horror and destruction awaited them.

The United States tried to stay neutral and not choose sides in the war. But the sinking of the *Lusitania* radically changed Americans' opinions. President Wilson kept hoping for a peaceful end. But in early 1917, the Germans sank several American cargo ships. Then Germany urged Mexico to invade the U.S., promising to return land in several southwestern states to Mexico. President Wilson finally decided it was time to get involved. The United States entered the war on April 6, 1917.

When it was over, the United States emerged as the dominant world power. It could not sit back any longer and isolate itself from world problems. Other governments would look to the U.S. for help and advice with their conflicts in the future.

World War I was called "the war to end all wars." But it didn't. Twenty years later, Europe was once again engulfed in a multi-country war. Wars now had to be numbered. The next one was called World War II.

One of the social changes that got a boost from the outbreak of war was the women's movement. Women had been trying for years to gain the right to vote. They finally won it on June 4th, 1919 when Congress passed the Nineteenth Amendment to the Constitution.

Another change involved the growing number of women who wanted to work outside the home. As men left to fight the war in 1917, women took over their jobs. Besides working as secretaries and phone operators, they also stepped into jobs as mechanics, streetcar conductors, painters and elevator operators. About 11,000 women joined the Navy as stenographers and clerks.

For better or for worse, life in homes across America and around the world began to change.

About the Author

Marianne Olson is the granddaughter of Sara Lisa Melander, who made the adventurous journey back to Sweden in the summer of 1914. Although most of the story is pure fiction, many parts are based on true events. Marianne traveled to Sweden to visit the farm where her grandmother was born. The house and lands are still owned by family members. While there, she plucked a rock out of a stone wall, just like Joel did, so she could always keep a piece of Sweden close by her.

Marianne is the author of three other books for children, published under her married name, Marianne Mitchell. Her first book, *Maya Moon*, (Sundance Publishing, 1995) is a bilingual folktale from Mexico about the moon. Her other books include *Say It in Spanish!* (Teacher Ideas Press, 1997) and *Coo Coo Caroo* (Richard C. Owen Publishers, 1999). Many of her stories and articles appear regularly in children's magazines, such as *Highlights for Children, Pockets,* and *New Moon.* Marianne has won three awards from the editors of *Highlights.* Her story, "Windows of Gold," won the magazine's 1998 Fiction Contest.

Marianne lives in Tucson, Arizona with her husband, Jim and their two dogs.

To order additional copies of OVER THE WAVES, complete the information below:

Ship to: (please print)

Name_____

Address_____

City, State, Zip_____

Would you like the book autographed?   _____

If so, to whom?_____

_____ copies of OVER THE WAVES
@ $ 9.95 each $_____

Postage & handling: $1.50 per book $_____

Arizona residents add 5% sales tax $_____

Total amount enclosed $_____

Please make checks payable to: Marianne Olson

Send to: Marianne Olson
          Rafter Five Press
          P.O. Box 65618
          Tucson, AZ 85728